Text Classics

HELEN GARNER was born in 1942 in Geelong, and was educated there and at Melbourne University. She taught in Victorian secondary schools until 1972—when she was dismissed for answering her students' questions about sex—and then started writing journalism for a living.

Her first novel, *Monkey Grip*, was published in 1977, won the 1978 National Book Council Award and was adapted for film in 1981. Her second book, the two novellas *Honour & Other People's Children*, was published in 1980. Since then Garner has published novels, short stories, essays, feature journalism and long-form non-fiction.

In 1995 she published *The First Stone*, a controversial account of a Melbourne University sexual-harassment case. *Joe Cinque's Consolation* (2004) was a study of two murder trials in Canberra. Her account of the trial of Robert Farquharson, *This House of Grief* (2014), was a *Times Literary Supplement* Book of the Year and won the Ned Kelly Award for Best True Crime Book. Her most recent novel, *The Spare Room* (2008), was translated into many languages, and won a Victorian Premier's Literary Award, a Queensland Premier's Award and the Barbara Jefferis Award. *Everywhere I Look* (2016), a collection of short non-fiction, won the Australian Book Industry Award for General Non-fiction.

Garner has also won two Walkley Awards, in 1993 and 2017; the inaugural Melbourne Prize for Literature, in 2006; and the Windham-Campbell Prize for Non-Fiction, in 2016. She lives in Melbourne.

MICHAEL SALA lives in Newcastle. He was born in the Netherlands in 1975, and first came to Australia in the 1980s. His critically acclaimed debut, *The Last Thread*, won the 2013 NSW Premier's Literary Award for New Writing and was the regional winner (Pacific) of the 2013 Commonwealth Book Prize. His most recent novel, *The Restorer*, was shortlisted for the NSW and Victorian Premiers' Literary Awards for Fiction.

Honour &
Other People's Children
Helen Garner

textpublishing.com.au

Text Publishing Melbourne Australia

The Text Publishing Company acknowledges the Traditional Owners of the country on which we work, the Wurundjeri people of the Kulin Nation, and pays respect to their Elders past and present.

textclassics.com.au
textpublishing.com.au

The Text Publishing Company
Wurundjeri Country, Level 6, Royal Bank Chambers, 287 Collins Street, Melbourne Victoria 3000 Australia

First published by McPhee Gribble Publishers, 1980.
This edition published by The Text Publishing Company, 2018.
Reprinted 2023.

Cover design by W. H. Chong
Typeset by Midland Typesetters

Printed and bound in Australia by Griffin Press, an Accredited ISO AS/NZS 14001:2004 Environmental Management System printer.

Print ISBN: 9781925603729
Ebook ISBN: 978192626711

CONTENTS

Testing the Voice
by Michael Sala

I FIRST encountered Helen Garner in a postgraduate creative writing class when I was twenty-four. I was working on a novel set in an undercooked version of medieval France— my way of writing about family without admitting it. With her arrival, this class, which I found tedious and vague, suddenly became interesting. Here was someone unafraid to be specific, to wade into someone's fifteenth draft and state what had to be done. She was a marvellous jolt of electricity that energised the class for the semester she was there.

I met Helen again years later, at a mutual friend's house, when I was leaving the debris of a marriage breakdown. She looked on as I summarised the situation to my friend. I couldn't read the expression on her face, but I remember thinking: Oh, what must Helen think of my hopelessly messy life?

I didn't read her works until later. To read *Monkey Grip* is to see the beginning of a whole subgenre of Australian writing—it's a novel held together by voice and concentrated vantage point, the granular detail of an urban Australian culture carried on in dingy kitchens and bedrooms, a work that shakes off the constraints of structure and plot in favour of sheer *presence*.

What then to make of Garner's second book? Is it, as Peter Craven observes, less vigorous but showing greater artistry? At first glance *Honour & Other Peoples' Children* might seem an interlude between the creative burst of *Monkey Grip* and the explorations of subject matter and vantage point of *The Children's Bach* and *Cosmo Cosmolino*—themselves stepping stones to Garner's pioneering position astride those two formerly distinct categories of fiction and journalism.

But there is far more to it than this. For me, to read Garner's fiction is to understand my own fascination with writing novels, to understand why I am doing what I am doing. She makes you do that—ask questions, see yourself and whatever it is that drives you in the act of reading her books.

Honour & Other Peoples' Children, as much as *Monkey Grip*, establishes Garner's formidable skills as a prose story-teller. But if *Monkey Grip* establishes the classic Garner voice—its directness, the finely rendered acuity of vantage point—*Honour & Other People's Children* vigorously tests that voice. As Bernadette Brennan notes in *A Writing Life: Helen Garner and Her Work*, Garner originally intended her second book to be a novel that replicated the style and subject matter of *Monkey Grip*. After struggle and failure, and a traumatic meeting with her publishers in 1978, Garner changed tack, 'picked the novel apart and fashioned it into two long stories.'

The work feels differently autobiographical to *Monkey Grip*, but not *less* so. The autobiographical elements seem to have been separated from one another and deployed in the various characters and relationships around which the two novellas are shaped. And shaped they are. These two works are classically structured in their broad narrative arcs. Garner's presence in the character Kathleen is obvious, but she seems to exist too in Ruth and Scotty: in Ruth's relationship to her children, in Scotty's verbal incisiveness, the way she draws on self-doubt for momentum. I read the conflict between Ruth and Scotty, in this sense, as a conflict between Garner and herself.

If the love in *Monkey Grip* is hopelessly intertwined with sex, then the love at the core of *Honour & Other Peoples' Children* is largely separate from it. These novellas are more about friendship.

In *Honour* this theme emerges through the relationship triangle of Kathleen, Frank/Flo and Jenny. That is, Frank and Flo form a kind of single dramatic unit in the story, inflecting and channelling a relationship between two women. Kathleen has long since left her husband, and the three of them—herself, Frank and Flo—have established a new dynamic. This has shifted with the arrival of Jenny, whose claims to Frank, and indeed Flo, encompass much of Kathleen's informal place in the family unit. Jenny wants Frank to divorce Kathleen so that *they* can marry.

Everything at the start of this novella is out of balance. What is needed is for Kathleen and Jenny to come to grips, to forge a new balance out of love, conflict and communication. Conflict, particularly in the domestic setting, is so often about miscommunication. A series of escalating territorial encounters culminate in an image in which I cannot help but see Helen Garner completely—Kathleen breaking into a house, transgressing boundaries just soft enough for things to get messy. But this is good. The break-in is exactly what's needed: the transgression disrupts and illuminates subtle boundaries and resentments, forcing Kathleen and Jenny to risk everything in their dialogue, enabling them to acknowledge some hopeful part of each other for the first time. The closing image of the novella captures this brilliantly: the two women balanced on a seesaw under Flo's watchful eye. Is this the end of the matter then? Has a new balance been achieved?

Perhaps the image is an illusory one. There is no *see* without *saw*. Early in the novella, Garner renders the image of a dog catching a ball, frozen momentarily in midair before the inevitable descent, the illusion of stasis. The point is that anything is possible: the means for friendship is there, but so is the means for its dissolution. Balance is a never-ending process.

Taking away the particulars, *Other Peoples' Children* develops the narrative, and mirrors it, so that we move again from a lack of balance to its rediscovery. Except this time the friendship between two women is accelerating towards dissolution. Garner sums it up near the end:

> So this was why people in real life screamed and broke things and grew violent: because the mind let go, and afterwards your body was as loose and

fine as a sleeper's, a dancer's, a satisfied lover's. You
were empty, all your molecules were harmoniously
realigned. You were skinned, liberated, wise. You
were out of reach.

By the final confrontation, the tools used to maintain the
friendship have been blunted. Furthermore, there is no
Flo/Frank character to provide a centre of gravity. Laurel,
related by blood only to Ruth, can be withdrawn from Scotty
at will. Alex as a housemate, and not related to anyone,
cannot perform the same role of interlocutor as Frank does
in *Honour*. The only sexual relationships occur on the
fringes, pulling Scotty and Ruth away from one another
and towards different cultural vantage points.

Ironically, Madigan and Denis, one artistic, the other
pragmatic, have a lot in common and perhaps represent some
of the limitations of second-wave feminism in Australia in
the 1980s. There is free love and birth control, but who is
getting the most out of this liberation? And underneath there
is still a rigid operation of gender within predetermined
roles: the women do the washing and the cleaning and the
cooking. The men are looked after and exert influence on the
women to suit their own interests. Both men are dependent
on the women in their lives but terrified of losing their
own freedom. Even the youngest male in the novella, the
boy Wally, instinctively (through the formative influence of
his absent father) exerts a disproportionate influence on the
females around him, disrupting his sister's life, consigning
her to menial supporting roles and doing his part to exac-
erbate the conflicts rupturing the friendship between Ruth
and Scotty.

The driving question for me is: What ultimately most causes the dissolution of Ruth and Scotty's relationship? Their friendship is a bond nurtured in the contemporaneous currents of feminism—and subjected to the same disruptive pressures.

One of those pressures, operating as a backdrop in both novellas—and a crucible for many of the forces that tear at the fabric of friendship and selfhood—is the notion of parenthood, its oppressive, illuminative, connective and transformative presence. Perhaps the most powerful line I have read in fiction about parenthood occurs early in *Honour*, when Kathleen spends a few days looking after her brother's children. After a quietly traumatic afternoon spent at the shops with a pair of boisterous toddlers, Kathleen is at her brother's house listening to them play outside: 'The little shovels made a damp grating sound as the children sank them into the sand.' Everything in parenthood is contained in that image: the intimate attention to detail, the domestic loneliness, the sheer, small, oppressive *repetitiveness* of that sound as it digs deeper into the quiet of the scene, deeper into the bruised consciousness of the exhausted parent, deeper, even as attention strains towards something larger. It is the sort of brilliant moment of perspective, economical and nuanced and deceptively rich, that characterises the breadth of Garner's work.

For Jennifer Giles

'...Things mattered
and love, anxious love
rose and put forth its flags.'

CHRIS WALLACE-CRABBE
*The Emotions Are Not
Skilled Workers*

Honour

On summer nights they walked through city gardens.

The air stood thick in their nostrils, a damp warmth lay upon their shoulders. Water dripped somewhere, randomly, without rhythm. On the other side of the banked plants people were murmuring idly in a foreign language. Jenny's head swam in the heat: her pores opened for the sweat to break. She saw his face floating by the fleshy flowers, eager, sharp and gentle. She wanted to take him in through her skin.

'What is that tree? What is that plant?' he asked her, and she told him the names. He did not try to remember them much, asked merely to hear her say the words in her English accent.

'How is it you know their names?'

'Oh, my father. And there are days,' she said, 'when the only things that don't look sad to me are plants.'

'Why are women so sad?' said Frank.

'I don't know,' she said. 'I don't think it's catching. Is that what you're worried about?' She stopped walking and looked him in the eyes. Behind her an iron fence with spikes rose up against the sky, which was deep blue with points of yellow light.

'Maybe,' he said after a moment. She was looking at him. One of her eyes was set very slightly higher than the other, as in some Cubist painting he may have once seen. He stepped off the path and cartwheeled lightly away over the springy grass. Once he had seen his daughter, on a sandbank in a desert, do fifty cartwheels in a row under moonlight.

*

When Kathleen answered the phone, Frank's sharp voice said,

'Hullo. It's me.'

Kathleen laughed out loud. Only a husband would announce himself thus.

'What?' he said.

'Nothing,' she said, sobering up.

'Listen. Can you come over tonight? I'd like to have a talk.'

'Anything wrong?'

'No. Just some stuff I'd like to clear up.'

*

4

The front door of the long house was left open for her and Frank was writing something in his violent, swooping hand at the kitchen table.

'Time one of you swept the hall,' she said from the doorway.

'Well, I won't be here much longer.' His cackling laugh rang out among the teacups hanging from their shelf. He sprang up nervously, took two big steps around the table and leaned against the stove with his bare arms crossed. He stared down at his feet with an assumed air of perplexity.

'Listen, Kathleen!' He leaped forward, gripped the table edge with both hands and leaned over it, but kept his face turned up to where she stood on the step. She noticed with a small shock that his hair was quite thickly grey at the sides. He narrowed his greenish eyes and stretched his thin mouth sideways like a man at the start of a hundred yard dash. The familiar drama caused her stomach to start trembling with the desire to laugh.

'Things have got to change! They can't remain the same!' he cried.

She laughed in confusion. 'What, Frank?'

'Sit down. Do you want a cuppa?' He would bounce wildly to the ceiling.

'You'd burn yourself. Spit it out.'

He gathered himself into a bunch and threw it at her. 'There's something I want. I want a divorce.'

He propped in front of the cupboard door, staring round at her to watch her cop it. She remembered suddenly how a dog they had once used to catch a thrown stick in his mouth—it stopped him dead at the moment of impact, *whack* between his black and pink jaws, but fitted: he regained his stride and ran on.

'See?' he burst out, pacing up and down with one forefinger laid against his cheek. 'It won't be any different between us. Just on paper.'

'But—what's put this into your head?'

She felt blankly curious, looking down at the bandy curves of his legs, brown and stringy in baggy khaki shorts.

'It wasn't *my* idea.' He spun round as if accused. 'Jenny wants me to—sort of—clean up my past.' His laugh was high-pitched, almost a giggle. He pulled his mouth down at the corners.

Kathleen turned blind with rage for two seconds. This time it took her a good moment to swallow it, spit from the caught stick. Frank squinted at her and suddenly the speed went out of him. He sat down at the table.

'That was a bit undiplomatic,' he remarked quietly, as if to an invisible audience.

She stared, blank as blotting paper.

'Come and sit down, Kath.'

She needed to, and obeyed.

There was a pile of papers, written on, between them on the table. Frank shifted his feet on the matting. A meek breeze came down the hall from the open front door, slid loosely across the papers and confounded itself with the warm air in which husband and wife sat. The top sheet of paper lifted as if to move sideways. Frank dumped the sugar bowl heavily on to the stack. In the fluorescent light the grains glittered.

'You see,' he began in a gentler voice, with his head on one side, 'I've always thought I'd go on being related to you, for the rest of my life.'

Normal existence began to tick steadily again. Someone had cleaned the louvre windows over the sink, and the panes gleamed darkly. In fact, the kitchen was full of shining surfaces. Frank was a great cleaner. When she was sick, even years after they had separated, he would burst into her room with broom, dust-pan and brush and whirl about like a winnowing wind, setting all to rights, placing objects in piles and at right-angles to each other.

'We will be, won't we? Related, I mean. Because Flo will relate us.'

'Yes.' His face turned soft at the name. 'But Jenny—well...she hasn't lived like we have all these years. "Smashing monogamy."' He laughed bitterly. 'She wants things to be resolved. "Resolved" is a word she uses a lot.'

'You don't mean you want to get *married* again?'

7

'If I do, it'll only be to get European work papers,' he said hastily.

'I thought one reason why we never got a divorce before was so we wouldn't make the same mistake again! Remember what you always used to say? "Getting married isn't something you do—it's something that happens to you."'

'That's true. The first time, anyway.'

She hung dangerously, as if the other half of a high-wire act had failed to show up for work. He looked down at his hands.

'You know one thing she's done for me—she's made me cut right back on my drinking.'

'How'd she do it? She must have something I haven't got.'

'I've been living like a maniac for five years, Kath. Not just when you shot through with Perfect-Features—but afterwards—doing nothing but work, drink and fuck—look at my hair!' Getting back into his stride, he indicated his grey temples with a gun-like gesture. 'Look at me! Thirty-two years old and grey as a church mouse!'

She laughed with a twist of the mouth.

'I've been bullshitting myself all these years,' he went on. 'I want a *real* place to live, with a backyard where I can plant vegies, and a couple of walls to paint, and a dog—not a bloody room in a sort of railway station!' Breathless with rhetoric, he sat smiling shyly at her, one arm resting on the tabletop.

'Does Jenny want that too?'

'Yes.' He might have blushed.

She would have to be mingy indeed to stay hard-faced against his hopefulness. 'What about Flo?'

'Jenny loves her. Can she come and live with us for a while? For a month or so? It would be a home. I'll drive her to school.' He looked eager, leaning over his arm.

'Does she want to go?' It was only a formality.

'Oh yes. I think so.'

Some half-gagged splinter-self in the depths was twisting in protest: what about *me*? but Kathleen kicked the door shut on it. There were no demands or protests she might rightfully make. He had always treated her honourably. In five years she had never given it one moment's conscious thought, but had lounged upon the unspoken assumption that she was still somebody's, even when she was most alone.

She looked up and saw a tiny liquid twinkling in the inner corner of Frank's left eye.

'Look!' he shouted, pointing to it. 'A tear! It is! I can still squeeze one out!'

*

Kathleen ran in from the glaring street. Through the screen door she perceived dim shapes moving at the other end of the passage. The wire smelled coldly

9

of rust as she pressed her nose to it and rattled her fist against the wood. Jenny was calling back over her shoulder as she approached the door.

'So I told her I considered my contract fulfilled,' she was saying in a tone of such dry resoluteness that Kathleen envied her a firm life: orderliness, self-esteem. She saw Kathleen and said, 'Oh!' They had never met, but stared at each other through the clotted wire with suddenly quailing hearts.

'I've just come for Flo,' said Kathleen.

'Would you like to come in? We're watching the news.'

Frank was hunched forward, elbows on knees. 'Come to check up on me, have you,' he said, not taking his eyes off the screen where a man's face opened and closed its mouth.

'Who's this clown?' said Kathleen, ignoring the jibe.

'Lang Hancock.'

'What's he on about?'

'Sssh!' said Frank. 'Watch and find out.'

'He claims,' said Jenny tactfully, 'that he flew through a radioactive cloud thirty years ago and that it didn't do him any harm—thus, that it's all right to mine uranium. A fine piece of Australian political reasoning.'

'But who's the woman?'

'His daughter. He's brought her along to show that his genes didn't suffer.'

10

'What! He reckons he didn't suffer genetic damage, and that's his *daughter*, with that huge polka dot *bow* round her neck?' Kathleen started to giggle.

Frank turned round crossly and said, 'Sssh, will you? This is serious!'

Kathleen put her beach towel over her mouth and pulled a chastised face. She picked up a newspaper and flipped through it.

'My God,' she said. 'It says here that a lady went into hospital in France to have a baby, and when she came out of the anaesthetic they'd cut one of her *hands* off.'

Frank switched off the television. 'Do you ever read the actual news, Kath? Apart from Odd Spots, death notices and so on?'

'Of course,' said Kathleen, obviously bluffing.

Jenny stared at her, and thought in a vague blur of fear, 'Is it being a mother that makes her head racket round like that? Will this happen to me?'

The two women sat in similar poses, limbs arranged so as to appear casual. They did not perceive their striking similarity; they both made emphatic hand gestures and grimaces in speech, stressed certain words ironically, cast their eyes aside in mid-sentence as if a sustained gaze might burn the listener. Around each of them quivered an aura of terrific restraint. If they both let go at once, they might blow each other out of the room.

11

'This is a nice house,' said Kathleen recklessly. 'Why doesn't Frank just move in here, instead of both of you having to look for another place?'

The air bristled.

'Because then he would be living at my place,' enunciated Jenny carefully, 'and we would like to start off on equal terms.'

'We've found a place, anyway,' said Frank.

'I'll give you a hand to move then, whenever you like,' Kathleen charged on. There was a short hush.

'Will you have a beer, Kathleen?' said Jenny.

'No thanks. I was going to take Flo for a swim.'

'It's a scorcher, all right,' said Frank, shifting in his chair.

Light filtered through drawn curtains, the three characters floated in watery dimness. Pale objects burned: cotton trousers, a dress faded as a flour bag, a flash of eye-white in a turned head. There was a faint smell of lemon.

Flo ran in, dragging a white dog by its collar.

'I heard you talking, Kath. See? This is Jenny's dog. She *loves* me.'

'I bet she does. Come on—we'll go to the baths.'

'Come into my room and get your things, Flo,' said Jenny.

Flo took Kathleen's hand. 'Come and look at Jenny's things. She's got jewels, and a special thing like scissors for your eyelashes.'

The brown floor in the passage creaked under them. Jenny snapped on a lamp in the front room and the heavy double bed sprang into the light. Flo edged her way round its obtrusive foot to reach the treasure box by the empty fireplace. The two women stood awkwardly, embarrassed by the meaning of the bed, but Flo turned round with a tweezer-like object in her hand and applied it brusquely to her eyelashes.

'Careful!'

'See? They make your eyelashes *curly*.'

Jenny laughed and flicked a glance at Kathleen to see if she disapproved. Kathleen did, but was also curious, and looked to see if Jenny had used the tool on her own eyes, which were brown and unevenly set.

'When are you coming here to spend the night, Flo?' said Jenny.

Flo looked shyly at her mother, not wanting to make her jealous. 'Can I, one day?'

'Of course.'

'I'll phone you,' said Jenny.

Jenny and Flo took a step towards one another and Flo raised her arms as if to kiss her goodbye. They both stopped at the same instant and looked at Kathleen with identical expressions: waiting for dispensation. Kathleen smiled and nodded, they were released and kissed smackingly.

Outside the front door the hot afternoon enfolded them in its dry blanket. The gate disturbed vegetation and set free a dizzying wave of privet smell and the peppery scent of pink climbing roses.

Halfway down the lane Frank caught up with them and took hold of Flo's other hand.

'Hang on, Kath! I've got something to ask you. Don't you ever walk slowly?'

'No. Do you?'

'No.' He fell into step beside Flo. 'I'd like to be able to saunter. I read that in a book of aphorisms: "It is a great art to saunter." Anyway I have to go down to Mum and Dad's.'

'Is anything wrong down there?'

'Mum's a bit under the weather.'

'What? Why didn't you tell me?'

'I only found out last night. Dad rang up. Poor old blighter can hardly see to dial the number.'

'What's actually wrong with Shirl?'

'I don't know. Some sort of nervous complaint. Quite painful. She's had the doctor.' He lashed savagely at a hedge. 'I don't think Dad can manage by himself. He's never asked me for help before.'

They walked along in silence.

'Do you want me to come down with you?' said Kathleen. 'Unless you're taking Jenny, of course.'

'Would you? It'd get the load off me a bit. They haven't met Jenny yet. Mightn't be the moment to break that one to them.'

'Can I come?' Flo inserted the request purely for form's sake.

14

'No,' said Kathleen. 'You can't miss school. You can stay home with the others.'

'Well, can I go and live with Frank and Jenny in their new house, then?' She was only flying a kite, barely listening for the answer, lining up her sandal toes with the cracks of the footpath so that the end of each fence fell upon an even number.

'Yes. If you want to.' Kathleen was trying to smile.

Flo seized her round the waist with her wiry arms. 'But what if you miss me too much? You won't cry or anything, will you?'

Her teeth were uneven and her forehead at this anxious moment displayed five horizontal lines of wrinkles so exactly like Frank's that Kathleen was all at sea.

'I can come and visit you,' she said. 'You can invite me over for dinner and we can both cook.'

Kathleen looked up from this bony embrace and saw Frank leaning against the fence with a strange smile on his face. 'He must be happy,' she thought. Flo pranced about. The parents' faces were stiff and their expressions inappropriate. Kathleen felt old, and perhaps bitter, but not against these two creatures whose separateness from herself, no matter how many times it had been demonstrated, she could never really bring herself to believe in.

*

Frank and Kathleen stood side by side like children in the doorway. Shirley was asleep, her head turned sharply to one side on the pillow, her mouth open as if she had just cried out.

'The doctor says it's called psoriasis,' offered Jack in the kitchen. 'She sleeps most of the time.' He smiled helplessly at them, bewildered, wanting to be appeased and approved of. Age had shrunk him, and he hardly reached Frank's shoulder.

'What's the doctor giving her? I mean—she shouldn't be knocked out like that, should she?' Frank moved agitatedly about the room, pulling open cupboard doors and slamming them again without looking inside.

'Blowed if I know, Frankie,' said the old man. His knotty hands were resting on the back of a chair. 'The doctor's a young chap, 'bout your age. I s'pose he knows what he's talking about.'

'I wouldn't be so bloody sure. They're drug-happy, those blokes—eh, Kath?'

She nodded, watching.

'I was just going to wake her up and give her something to eat, when you two arrived,' said Jack. 'I had a snack a little while ago.' On the sink were a plate, a knife and a fork, rinsed.

'I'll do it, Dad,' said Frank. 'You sit down there and take a break. What'll we give her, Kath?'

They cobbled together a dish of yoghurt and fruit, and Frank took it into the bedroom. Jack, legs crossed in his favourite corner chair, deerstalker cap pulled down over his bristly eyebrows and transistor whining faintly on his lap, began a soft tuneless whistle, tapping his fingertips on the armrests and looking out the window with elaborate casualness.

'Tum te tum te tum. Well...' he murmured. He sneaked a look at Kathleen and returned to his contemplation of a bush outside the glass.

'Think I'll pop out the back for a sec and have a look at the garden before it gets too dark,' said Kathleen at last, to put him out of his misery.

'Mmmm...there's quite a show out there. Pick some to take home.' One foot in its gleaming brogue beat rhythmically on air.

She made her escape and stood in mild air on the sloping lawn. A wind moved in the garden, very gentle and sweet: it shifted pleasantly among the leaves of small gums and roses past their season. The sky blurred upward, pearly as the inside of a shell, and in this delicate firmament there floated a perfect moon, its valleys and mountains lightly etched.

Shirley's voice rose sharply from the bedroom, and Frank's answered. Their words were indistinct. Then footsteps thumped, and Frank burst out the back door and stood staring desperately into the massed hydrangeas. Kathleen stepped up beside him.

'I had to feed her with a spoon,' he said, grinding his teeth and sniffing. 'She didn't want me to. She only wants Dad.'

'She's probably ashamed.'

'What? What of?'

'Being weak in front of you. And she's probably worried about being ugly.'

'Ugly! I don't give a damn about that! I just want to know what drugs those bastards have got her on. I've never seen her as dopey as this!' He clenched his fists and let out a sob. Kathleen slipped one arm round his waist and tried to hug him unobtrusively. He was rigid and very thin.

'Does she know I'm here?'

'Yes. Go and say hullo. I think she might want a drink. I'll stay out here and calm down.'

The old woman struggled to sit up. 'No, don't kiss me,' she said in distress, moving her head from side to side as Kathleen approached. 'I'm all—' She pulled her nightdress together at the neck to hide the scaly patches of skin on her chest. Jack smiled vaguely and felt his way along the wardrobe and out of the room.

'I've brought you a drink, Shirl.' Kathleen was all solidity and hearty tone, sticking her hand out with the fizzing glass in it. After two sips of dry ginger, great runs of air rumbled up from Shirley's stomach, and she turned her face away, blushing feebly and covering her mouth with her hand.

'I'm sorry,' she whispered.

'Makes you burp, does it,' said Kathleen. 'That's what fizzy drinks are for.'

'I hate it,' cried Shirley passionately, still with her shoulder turned.

'Do you? I love it,' said Kathleen without a shadow of a lie but full of motive. 'It's good for you.'

The bedclothes were all skew-whiff, the sheets out of alignment with the blankets, the whole lot dragging on the floor.

'Will I tidy up a bit for you, Shirl?'

'Oh, it's too much trouble, love.' She fretted among the pillows, turning her head in abrupt movements like a bird.

'No it's not. I'll call Frank.'

Frank settled his mother on a chair while Kathleen took hold of the bedclothes and yanked them away. A shower of silvery dead skin flakes flew out and fell in drifts on the polished wood floor.

'It's awful,' moaned Shirley, humiliated in her dressing-gown.

'Don't be silly, Mum,' said Frank. 'It's *not* awful, and you *must* accept being looked after.'

Kathleen worked away efficiently with clean linen, shoving her hands between mattress and base and plumping up pillows. She remembered sitting thinly on a chair with her feet dangling while her mother 'made her bed nice'.

'There you are. Hop in here. I'll run the old sheets through the machine.' She gathered them up in her arms and forged out the door.

19

Shirley's splintery voice trailed after her. 'The second cycle, lovey—don't forget to open both the taps, and not too much soap powder...'

'She knows how to *do* it, Mum,' snapped Frank. Kathleen almost laughed. When Frank and his mother talked like that, things were getting back to normal. She blundered round in the laundry, unused to machines that worked without the introduction of coins, and got the thing going at last. She was standing there thinking in the cloth-muffled room when Frank slipped in and shut the door behind him.

'What's Jack up to?' said Kathleen.

'Fumbling round in the study trying to find Mum's prescription.'

Frank picked up a basket full of pegs and rattled it fiercely. 'I think this is probably the beginning of the...race to the end.' He grimaced, pointed one finger heavenwards and then down to the earth, and mimed sleep as children do, eyes closed and palms together under one cheek. They both laughed painfully.

In Shirley's kitchen the autumn sunlight was oblique and very bright. Kathleen squinted and moved constantly from one part of the room to another in search of an area of shade for her face. There was a blinding sheen on the table-boards, shafts of light sprang from cutlery, Frank's hair stood out like an aureole. The plastic cover of the photo album dazzled relentlessly.

'Look,' said Frank.

'I can't see.'

'It's my dog, a foxy I had when I was a kid.'

Shuffling footsteps came along the passage, and Shirley stood in the doorway with a mustard-coloured shawl wrapped round her.

'What are you doing out of bed, Mum?'

'Oh…I'm all right,' she insisted in her cracked voice, pushing past him and sitting down at the table. 'I'd rather be up and about.'

Frank clicked his tongue, but passed her the album. 'Look, Mum. Remember when Auntie Hazel used to stay in her caravan in our back yard?'

Shirley seized the album and shielded her eyes over it. 'Oohoo, that Hazel,' she crooned with a note of malice.

'Look at that dress she's got on! We said at the time, Brocade's as dead as a dodo, we said. We all knew what she was after when she latched on to Keith. There was the house in Kyneton, all his mother's things, you never saw such lace—and the furniture, a cheval glass she'd had made up for her by an old Chinaman up Ballarat way…Hazel hung on like grim death, but she only got hold of it a clock here, a chair there.' She turned the pages with a sigh, and they sat listening, half-hypnotised as she murmured. 'Ah, there's Jack as a younger man. He had a finely turned ankle in those days. It was the first thing I noticed about him. Why should I tell you all this? Dear God, it's life, I suppose.'

'I've got something to tell *you*, Mum,' said Frank suddenly. Kathleen looked up startled and saw him take the deep breath before the plunge.

'What, love.' Shirley hovered over the grey snaps like a map-reader.

'Kath and I are getting a divorce.'

The plastic page flopped loosely under her idle hand, as if she had not heard.

'Now, we don't want you to get *upset* about this, Mum,' he said, his voice sharpening into the old warning note.

'What, lovey?' She turned the book sideways and bent over it the better to scrutinise.

'I might be getting *married* again, Mum. I'm going to *live* with someone.'

Shirley looked up from the picture book and spoke very clearly, with a note of world-weariness that they had never heard before. 'Oh, I don't give a damn. She can come down here. That couch turns into a double bed. I only ever wanted you, Kath, and Flo, but it's no use growling. I can't be worried about it now. Bring her down.'

Frank was shocked. Not only had he expected her to be outraged, but he needed her to be, so that he might define himself against her protest. It was perhaps the moment of his growing up. Before Kathleen's eyes

22

the knot dissolved, and she watched him float free, feet groping, full of alarm.

Kathleen and Frank went walking down by the shore, under the avenues of huge cypresses rooted deep in the sandy ground. Perhaps they would have liked to walk arm in arm: there were historical reasons for the fact that they did not.

'I love it here,' said Frank. 'It seems so old. I bet Yalta on the Black Sea must be like this—flat and mournful. When I read *The Lady with the Dog* I imagined it happening here.'

On the pier their footsteps rang hollow and water slapped way below. Long ships, business-like, slid past on their way to the heads: some quality of absence in the air brought them unnaturally close. It was late afternoon, and a strange metal light intensified most vividly the dark greens and greys of the shore, and of the sad water that seemed to stream past them oceanwards. Frank, absorbed in his Chekhovian fantasy, planted himself squarely at the very end of the pier, slitting his eyes and loosening his coat to let it flap in the wind.

'There's going to be a storm,' remarked Kathleen in a neutral tone, absent-mindedly brushing dandruff off his shoulders.

'Have you no eyes, Kathleen?' trumpeted Frank. He fronted the brisk wind with a histrionic gesture. 'Look about you! Is there no poetry left in your soul?'

'Oh, I think there might be a bit left,' she said drily. She stared past him.

The water was lashing at the encrusted supports of the pier, and the big lifeboat groaned on its pulleys. Their hair streamed back off their skulls and rain began to sprinkle sharply on to their upturned faces.

'Let's go, Frankie.'

'OK,' he grumbled good-naturedly, 'you old prune. I wish Floss was here. *She'd* play with me.'

They turned up their collars and let the wind hurry them back towards the car. On the dashboard Frank had sticky-taped a type-written notice which read, *This car should last another ten years*. He drove with nervous efficiency. As he drove he sang, accompanying himself with sharp taps of the left foot:

> *There's a trade we all know well*
> *It's bringing cattle over*
> *On every track to the Gulf and back*
> *Men know the Queensland drover*

and she joined in the chorus because she knew it would give him pleasure:

> *Pass the billy round boys*
> *Don't let the pintpot stand there*
> *For tonight we drink the health*
> *Of every Overlander*

Loudly and in harmony they sang, sneaking each other embarrassed, happy smiles, then laughed and avoided each other's eyes.

'I'm scared Dad'll go before I can get his story out of him,' said Frank.

'Didn't you start taping it?'

'Yes. But it's so hard to get him going. He's shy, and he gets mixed up.'

'Did you get the one about the carrot?'

Frank knitted his brows and mimicked his father's slow, musing voice: 'I was sitting on the verandah after work when Reggie Blainey came down the road dragging over his shoulder what looked like a *young sapling*. He got closer and I saw it was actually the fronds of a *giant carrot*. I says, Well, Reggie, that's the biggest carrot *I've* ever seen! And he looks up at me and he says, Listen, you reckon this is big? I dug for three hours—and the bloomin' thing forked at twenty foot.'

Under the rain, the lights of Geelong were coming on as they sped down the Leopold Hill.

*

Kathleen's brother-in-law opened the door to them in a flustered moment. An invisible child was throwing a tantrum in the kitchen, and from the stereo in the living room a string quartet was straining away loudly.

'Hul–lo!' he cried in amazement. 'What a treat! Come in! Pin was whizzed into hospital straight after lunch—the baby's overdue. We're just waiting for news.'

They followed him into the kitchen, where the benches and tables were covered in bright blue formica and the small window looked out over fruit trees and a chook pen. At their appearance the child on the floor ceased to beat his fists and sat up to stare, his cheeks puce and tear-stained.

'My goodness!' said Charlie. 'I haven't seen you two together for—must be five years! There's not a reconciliation, is there?' He clapped his hand over his mouth as if he had made a gaffe. Kathleen and Frank, whose lack of interest in divorce had given them a certain bohemian status in both their families, remained collected. Kathleen swept a mass of blocks off a chair and sat down. The two men stood about, Charlie flipping a teatowel, Frank grinning at the floor. The older boy appeared in the doorway as the string quartet reached its climax and resolved itself into one drawn-out, quivering harmony. Silence. Charlie sighed voluptuously.

'Wonderful, isn't it,' he said.

'When's mummy coming home. I want mummy to come home.'

'Yes dar–ling,' sang Charlie irrelevantly on two notes, his mind on something else but not soon enough, for a covered saucepan erupted on the stove and milk went everywhere. 'Damn. Blast it.'

Kathleen spoke up without forethought. 'I could stay for a few days, if you like, and give you a hand with the kids.'

'Oh, would you?' He spun round with the inadequate wettex dripping on his shoes.

'Am I neurotic?' thought Kathleen, already aware of a trickle of regret behind the smile.

She hurried the trolley along the bright shelves of the supermarket, Ben trotting at her side and Tom lording it in the seat above the merchandise. No matter how fast she moved, something horrible kept pace with her, ran smoothly along behind the ranged and perfect shining objects: something to do with memory, with time past she thought she had escaped, as long ago as childhood when she had striven to imagine her mother's life and her own future: meals, meals, meals: the meal as duty, as short leash, as unit of time inexorable into everlastingness. She dared not glance at other women passing lest she see confirmation of it in their faces. There was no word for this sickness in her, running alongside her, but *void*.

In the checkout queue she realised she had forgotten fruit.

'Will you stay here and mind the shopping while I run back?' Ben gripped her hand convulsively.

'I won't be long,' she pleaded. 'There's nothing to worry about—we'll go home and have some lunch.'

She wrenched herself free and bolted along the slick alleyways, frantic to be by herself even for sixty seconds. She glanced back at them as she skidded round the great cabinets steaming with frost and saw Ben's pale face eyeing her and Tom's mouth opening to let out one of his leisurely roars. *I can't stand it, can't stand it*, a whining chipmunk voice began up in the back of her skull, it chattered at her, jibbered, she dived both hands into the pile of netted oranges, flipped them this way and that, mould whiffed at her, *the skull beneath the skin* pipped the voice, *shit shit shit*, two bags at sixty-five cents, she counted on her fingers a dollar thirty something, now where are those two little buggers? God help them, God send me back to Flo, how did I stand it when she was only two? Only three more days and I'll be on that train.

Outside, she trundled the pusher up the hill. It was quicker to carry Tom in it than to round him up on foot, but he was fat and the heavy shopping bags, one in each hand against the handle of the flimsy pusher, bumped clumsily against her legs and the wheels as she progressed. Ben gripped the handle, continually swinging the triple load out of line. She fought herself for patience. The sky was thick, big drops started, they had no coats. Tom began to bellow,

'Wet! Wet! Wet! Wanna det out!'

28

'Oh shut up Tom!' she raged, wrenching hard to get the pusher wheel out of a crack in the pavement. Ben slid her a sly look.

'Will I shove a jelly bean into him?' he hissed.

They began to laugh conspiratorially.

'Where did you get 'em?'

'While you were paying the lady.'

The pathetic cavalcade struggled up the hill.

She sat on the back verandah cutting slice after slice off a rubbery ginger cake she had found in a tin and stuffing it into her mouth. The boys played in their sandpit. The sand was dark yellow but the rain had stopped. She remembered reading somewhere: only if you have been a child in a certain town can you know its sadness, bone sadness, sadness of the blood. *Every day the clouds come over.* She went and stood by the sandpit. The little shovels made a damp grating sound as the children sank them into the sand.

At teatime when Charlie came home from work, she served up for dessert a kind of pudding. Everyone but Tom ate it enthusiastically. Enthroned in his high chair, holding his spoon like a sceptre, he scowled into his bowl.

'Eat up, Tom,' said his father. He glanced at Kathleen and poked the pudding into a more attractive shape in the bowl. 'It's cake.'

Tom withered him with a look. 'That is *not cake.*' His aunt and his father lowered their lying heads on to the table among the plates and laughed in weak paroxysms.

The baby came, a girl. Kathleen sniffed the head of the creature rolled tightly in its cotton blanket. Looking at her sister had always been like looking into a mirror: large forehead, eyes that drooped at the outer corners, pointed chin, small mouth. Kathleen laughed.

'What's funny?' said Pin, shifting uncomfortably in the hospital bed.

'I was looking at your mouth. It's exactly the same as mine.'

'Small and mean,' said Pin, whose devotion to the church did not damp her vulgar sense of humour. 'Wanna see a cat's bum?' She pursed her lips into a tight bunch. They snickered in the quiet ward.

'You'll never go to heaven,' said Kathleen. 'You're rude.'

'Don't be a dill. Sit down here and tell me what you've been doing. The only way I can get away from the kids long enough to have a good talk with someone is by having another one.'

'Oh...I muck round. Read, you know. Clean up.'

'Charlie says Frank was down. You're not getting together again, are you?'

'Hardly. Too late for that, even if we wanted to.'

'What a shame. I always liked Frank.'

'So did I. Still do. I think he's the ant's pants. What've *you* been up to, apart from having babies?'

'Praying.' At Kathleen's polite attempt to conceal her disgust, Pin burst out laughing. 'I have—but I only said it to provoke.'

'How was the birth?'

'Oh, lovely. I mean—it would have been, if they'd left me alone. I was managing quite well, being a bit of an old hand, but I was probably making a lot of noise, because one of the doctors came in and mumbled something to the nurse, and next thing I know she's approaching with a big cheesy smile and one hand behind her back. Righto, Mrs Hassett! she says. I want you to curl up on the table with your bottom right out on the edge, just like a little bunny rabbit. No you don't! I said. No one's giving *me* a spinal—I was a nurse before I got like this. I *know* that bunny rabbit line—just get away from me, thanks very much. And I battled on, and voila!' She indicated with a flourish the sausage-shaped bundle in the cot beside the bed. 'Anyway, Kath—'scuse me for a sec. I'm going to stagger to the toilet.'

When Pin came back she was as white as a sheet.

'Is anything wrong?'

'I'm not sure. Here, help me back into bed, will you? I think I'd better call the doctor.'

'What, Pin?'

31

'I was wiping myself just now, and I felt something hard, right down in my vagina. I put my head between my knees and had a look. I think it's my cervix.'

They stared at each other. Pin tried to laugh. 'It's probably nothing.'

A nurse came. She slipped her hand under the bedclothes. Kathleen wandered over to the window and looked out over the grey bay with its stumpy palm trees and, further away towards Melbourne on the endless volcanic plain, the two dead mountains, rounded as worn-down molars.

The nurse said, 'I'll go and call doctor.' Her expression was respectful as she padded away on her soft white shoes. Pin grimaced and shrugged.

'Oh Pin. What a drag.' Kathleen sat down on the bed and took hold of her sister's hand with its heavy silver engagement and wedding rings. 'Are you still playing the piano?'

'Yes, and I'm getting better too.' Pin grinned defiantly. 'My teacher said, "For a thirty-five-year-old with a rotten memory, you're not doing too badly."'

Across her mouth flitted a stoicism, a setting of the lips, still well this side of martyrdom.

*

The house was at the bottom of a dead-end road with narrow yellowing nature strips, and a railway line running across its very end like stitches closing a bag. It was twelve o'clock and there was no one around.

Jenny came out the front door and saw Kathleen dawdling by her car, arm along brow against the strong sun. She looked small, dwarfed by the big blue day, and unusually hesitant, leaning there looking this way and that, squinting up her face so that her top teeth showed. Jenny felt a throb of almost sexual tenderness towards her: a hard spasm of the heart, a weakening in the pelvis. She darted out the gate and stopped in front of Kathleen, seized her wrist. With force of will she kept the other woman's hand, studied with a peculiar flux of love her sun-wrinkled eyes, the marks of her shrewd expressions. They could even smell each other: flower, oil, coffee, soap: and under these, warmed flesh, dotted tongue, glass of eye, glossy membrane, rope of hair, nail roughly clipped.

'Welcome,' said Jenny.

Perhaps they would never dare again. They stepped out of each other, frightened.

'There's nothing here to drink,' called out Frank on the verandah. 'I'm going to find a pub.'

Jenny turned away from Kathleen, distracted. 'I'll come with you.'

Kathleen waited, still leaning against her car, until they were out of sight, walking slowly in the heat with their arms round each other. Two ragged nectarine trees fidgeted their leaves in the scarcely-moving air.

Her head was faint in the dryness. She heaved herself up and turned to tackle the house.

Its facade, a triangle on top of a square, was slightly awry and painted the aqua colour favoured by Greek landlords. She ducked under an orange and green blind rolled up on rotted ropes at the outer edge of the verandah, and turned the key in the handle-less front door. In the tilting hallway she walked quickly past two or three small rooms with brown blinds half-drawn and opened the door into the kitchen, in which a combustion stove, painted white to indicate its decorative status, crouched in the chimney place, superseded by a gas cooker, itself forty years old, standing in a nearby corner alcove. Someone had slung a blanket across the window on two nails to keep the hot day out: its woollen folds muffled all movement of air and absorbed the knock of her footsteps.

She stood still in the bare centre of the room, on boards, in dimness. The heat was breathless. A drop of water bulged and quivered under the tap.

The back door was shut. It was made of four vertical strips of timber, also painted white, and closed with a loose brass knob. The timber had worn thin top and bottom, like the business end of front teeth, so that the dry brightness off the concrete outside was felt in the room as two insistent, serrated presences of light.

She opened the door, stepped down into the dazzling yard, and walked along by the grey wooden fence and through the green, dried-out trellis door into the wash-house with its squat copper and pair of troughs under the window never meant to open. She placed her palms lightly on the edge of the troughs. They were grey, forever damp and cool, clotted of surface and rimmed lead-smooth in paler grey; she had been bathed when very small in troughs such as these, and her mother had let her play with the wooden stick that she used to stir the copper, a stick with a face on the knob. The wash-house smelled of wet cloth and blue bags, and she could not climb out of the high trough by herself, so she was obliged to sit there nipple-deep in cooling water waiting for her mother, gazing blankly out the blurred window panes to the corner next to the dunny where the tank stood on its wooden stand, up to its ankles in grass even in summer, and if you tapped its wavy sides it would not give out a note for it was full to a level higher than you could reach, and its water was clear and swirly with wrigglers, baby mosquitoes that would not hurt you if you guzzled fast enough, and she sang out, 'Mu–um! I've finished' but her mother did not hear, for she was outside in the yard at the clothes line putting a shirt to her mouth to see if it was dry enough to be unpegged and taken in for ironing.

A bike clattered against the front fence.

'Kath–leen!' shouted Flo.

Kathleen slipped out of the wash-house and half-way down the yard came upon a rotary clothes-line rusting away on an angle, a skivvy faded to sand-colour hanging by one wrist from its lowest quadrant, like a flag left tattered and forgotten after a rout. She took hold of the body of it and, without thinking, raised it to her lips in that gesture of mothers, breathed in its sweet dry weathered cotton soapy perfume; and at that moment saw a to-and-fro movement behind the wash-house window panes. It was Flo waving to her.

She dropped the skivvy and plunged on towards the back fence, beyond which dizzy cicadas raved endlessly in trees bordering the railway line. The faint voices of Flo and Frank, a little duet for piccolo and banjo, were still behind her in the back of the house. She stood at the end of the yard, almost off the property. A door banged somewhere else, water ran loudly into a metal container, fat hissed in another kitchen. The sky, without impurity, went up for miles.

It was the house of her childhood. She knew its impermanent, camp-like feeling. When front and back doors were open, the house would be no more than a tunnel of moving air. Under rain, its roof would thunder and its downpipes rustle as you turned in your sleep. Heat in winter would have to be generated inside and cunningly trapped, in summer repulsed by crafty arrangements, early in the morning, of curtains and blinds. Unlike stone or brick, its weatherboard walls would not absorb the essence of its inhabitants' existence: they were as insubstantial as Japanese screens: disappointment and anxiety, hope and contentment would pass through them with equal ease and rapidity. The house laid no claim to beauty. It was humble, and would mind its own business.

The last piece of furniture to be persuaded through the narrow front door was an oval table missing all four castors. They worried it into the kitchen, pulled up chairs and sat around it.

'Didn't this used to be our dining-room table back at Sutherland Street, Frank?' said Kathleen.

'Yep. Four dollars at the Anchorage, remember? That was when I cornered the market in cane chairs, too.'

'Come off it! We only had three.'

'Yes, but the price had doubled by the following Saturday.'

The fridge was already whirring behind the door. Jenny passed out cans of beer and sat down next to Frank. He smiled at her, but Kathleen's opening line had launched him on a tide of domestic memory and he was away.

The impromptu performances that Frank and Kathleen put on at kitchen tables and other public places were the crudest manifestation of the force-field that hummed between them: an infinity of tiny signals—warning, comfort, rebuke—flashed from one to the other ceaselessly and for the most part unconsciously. In its most highly coded form it passed unobserved in a general conversation; in public garb it called others to witness, embraced them as audience or participants in embroidered tales of a common past. It was hatred, regret, pity; it was respect and the fiercest loyalty. They could no more have turned it off than turned back time.

Jenny was left striving for grace, for a courteous arrangement of features while they recited, delighted in the ring of names without meaning for her. Frank put his arm round her bare shoulders, but she kept looking at her beer can and fiddling it round and round, letting her curly hair fall across her face to shield her. There was a short silence in the room, during which Flo could be heard splattering the hose against the side wall of the house. They had opened the door and taken down the blanket as the afternoon drew on and the sun shifted off the concrete outside the kitchen, but the heat was still intense.

'Give the concrete out here a bit of a sprinkle, love,' Frank shouted. Flo did not answer, but a great silvery rope of water flew past the open door and whacked against the bedroom window.

'Down a bit! Down! Don't wet all our stuff!'

The dog, saturated and hysterical, darted into the kitchen and ran about in a frenzy. At the same instant they heard the first signs of life from next door, a rat-tat-tat of voices in a language they did not understand.

'Is that Greek?' said Jenny.

'Might be.' Frank was absent-mindedly stroking her neck. His dreamy smile sharpened into a cackle of laughter. 'Hey Kath—remember Joe and Slavica?'

'Oh God.' She turned to Jenny. 'They were a Yugo-slavian couple who lived next door to us when we were first married.'

'We got on fine with them for a while. They used to ask us in for dinner and force us to drink till we were falling off the chairs. We'd sing all night, it was great.'

'Yes, but poor Slavica,' said Kathleen. 'She didn't even score a place at the table. We'd arrive and there'd be three places set. Slavica would be out in the kitchen like a servant.'

'You mean—she actually *ate* out there?'

'Standing up. We used to have to drag her in and make her sit down.'

The two women exchanged their first straight look of solidarity. Frank galloped onwards, heading for the drama of it.

'Anyway, Joe got crazier. He used to come home from work with half a dozen bottles and drink the lot all by himself in front of the TV.'

'About ten o'clock one night we heard him start to curse and smash things—'

'Their little boy nicked over our back fence to hide.'

'He couldn't speak English. He let me cuddle him.'

39

'And then we heard the back door crash, and Slavica was locked out in the yard. She called out to us very softly, and we passed the kid back over the fence.'

'He didn't want to go back.'

'And straight away we heard Joe rush out into the yard and abuse her—'

'He *thumped* her!'

'And he dragged the kid inside and left her in the yard all night, she told us later. She slept in a corner near the chook pen.'

'Didn't you *do* anything?' said Jenny, horrified.

'*We* were scared of him, too!' said Frank. 'He was big! He was a maniac! We rang the police, but they didn't want to know about it—a domestic.'

Frank was on his feet now, his narrow eyes alight with story-teller's fervour. 'But one night Kath was driving home and she caught this ghostly figure in the headlights. It was Slavica running across the road with no shoes on. He'd kicked her out in the street. So Kath brought her into our place and she slept on the couch.' He made two stabbing motions with his fore-finger towards the living room. 'That couch in there, the white one. She said he was crazy because he suspected her of having an affair with the lodger. How corny can you get?'

'The lodger was a classic. A real lounge lizard. He gambled all his money away and couldn't pay the rent. He had a pencil moustache, slicked back hair, the lot.'

'Well, next morning we waited till Joe went to work and then sneaked out to see if the coast was clear. It was raining, and there were all the lodger's pathetic belongings chucked out on the footpath—a tattered suitcase, a pair of pointy two-tone shoes, a couple of lairy shirts—'

'Slavica dashed in and got the kid,' said Kathleen. 'I took them down to the People's Palace.'

'The Salvation Army?'

'We didn't know where to take them, and it wasn't safe at our place.'

'But wasn't there a Halfway House or something?'

'Not back then!' said Kathleen. 'This is Australia, mate!'

'Oh.'

Frank was poised to continue, bouncing on the balls of his feet. 'Anyway, Kath found her a room in a house in Northcote run by an older Yugoslavian who said she'd been through the same story, and on Saturday morning Kath drove Slavica home to pick up some kitchen things.'

'I pulled up out the front in this old VW we had at the time, and Slavica ran in and came out with an armful of pots and pans. She was too scared to go back for her clothes. Joe was on the front verandah with this terrible smile on his face, his arms were folded and he'd laugh—God it was awful, a sort of mad, bitter cackle— I said, Get in, Slavica, we have to get out of here.

She jumps in, I'm trying to start the flaming car, the kid in the back with eyes as big as mill-wheels—and at the last minute Joe comes tearing out with a long piece of string and a saucepan, and ties it on the back bumper bar, like people do at weddings.'

'My God.'

'I get the car into gear, he's raving and shriek-ing and half the street's hanging over their front gates watching—and just as we take off he gives the back of the car an almighty kick, and away we go with the saucepan rattling behind us. Talk about an undigni-fied retreat! I stopped about four blocks away and tore it off.'

Kathleen, out of breath, laughed nervously and glanced at Frank, who took up the tale. 'Well, so Slavica was OK, but from then on we got no rest at night. He'd drink himself off the map after work, then at ten o'clock he'd start this awful yelling.'

'Not yelling, exactly.' said Kathleen. 'Worse. More like loud whispering. Right under our bedroom window, which fortunately was on the first floor.'

'What did he say?'

She mimicked it slowly and dreadfully. '"Austra-lian—bitch—cunt. I make you trouble. I burn. I kill." And so on.'

There was a silence.

'Was I born then, Kath?' said Flo from the door. She was holding the dripping hose in her hand, and

42

the dirt round her mouth made her look as if she were grinning.

'You were born all right,' said Kathleen. 'You slept in a basket, and we were so scared of him that we kept you in our room all night, just in case. Point the hose the other way.'

'In fact,' said Frank, 'we were so scared of him that *I* started drinking too.'

'Is *that* why you started?' said Jenny dryly.

'I kept a sort of wooden club thing on the shelf above the front door.'

'And you used to prowl around the house brandishing it and saying—'

'"*He's strong, but I'm clever!*"' The ex-couple chorused it and burst into a roar of laughter.

'Why doesn't Jenny tell a story now?' said Flo, carefully directing the dribbling hose down her leg and off her ankle on to the concrete.

Faces relaxed, a softer laugh ran round the table, Jenny let her shoulder lean against Frank's and turned up her face towards Kathleen. They were, after all, people of good will.

Soon Frank and Flo wandered outside to inspect the site of the vegetable garden and the two women sat shyly at the table, touching the same boards with their bare soles, the same table-top with their forearms, but clumsy, a thousand miles from the moment of blessing which had united them that morning.

Jenny spoke. 'I was—'

'Frank's mother gave us those willow pattern plates,' gabbled Kathleen, without hearing her. 'You haven't met Shirley, have you? I'm glad you've got my old kitchen cupboard. It used to belong to my best friend when *she* was married. And those knives, see where they're engraved JF? Those are my grandfather's initials.'

Jenny, sick of it and too polite, fell back. What hope was there? Tongues were wagging stumps before such entanglement, such opaqueness of desire.

Out the back, in the long sun of late afternoon, Frank and Flo saw a bird hop extravagantly off the concrete, with a worm in its beak. They laughed, and with one accord folded their arms wing-like behind their backs and mimicked its irresistible self-satisfaction.

Flo in baby's bonnet and mosquito bites; Frank bearded like a Russian and wearing a sheepskin coat; Kathleen looking embarrassingly plain, her hair pulled back harshly off her forehead, her mouth drooping ill-temperedly; Frank chest-deep in a swimming pool with Flo perched on his shoulder; Kathleen squinting suspiciously, walking away from the camera with a huffy turn of the shoulder, standing awkwardly against bare asphalt in a silly mini-skirt. Then Frank and Kathleen grinning carelessly, open-faced and confident, audacious almost, shoulder to shoulder as if nothing would ever trouble the effortless significance of their being a couple.

Jenny shuffled the photos back into their box and knelt there among the cartons. Which was worse? Her utter non-existence at that moment when they had been happy, or her twinge of pleasure at Kathleen's plainness? She was disgusted with herself. She slid out the painful photo again and indulged the pang, like a child shoving its tongue against a loose tooth. She turned the photo over and read *Perth February 1970* in a round slanting hand. In February 1970 she had had no meaning to them, neither flesh nor spirit, no voice, no form. She was nebulous. She wrestled with her anonymity, tried to force herself into premature, retrospective existence. Serenely there on the glossy sheet they laughed up at her, brown-faced. Their being flowed oblivious beyond her. It was as outrageous to her spirit as if she had tried to imagine life continuing after her own death.

'Snoopers never find out anything nice,' said Frank behind her.

She jumped and shoved the picture away as if it had burned her.

'I used to snoop on Kath's diary, years ago,' he said. 'Know what the worst thing about it was? I never even got a mention.' He laughed out loud, cheerfully. 'Look. I brought you something.'

He held out his closed hand to her. Inside it something whirred loudly. She shrank back, dreading a prank, but he shook his head and kept proffering it to her.

'No. Look. It's a cicada.'

'Will it bite?'

'No. They sing!'

He opened his hand cautiously and took hold of the insect with thumb and forefinger. It goggled at her.

'*La* cigale et *la* fourmi! Par Jean de la Fontaine!' chanted Frank.

He was charming her, and she laughed. 'Let it go, Frankie. It might have a tiny heart attack.'

Lost in a dreamy curiosity, Frank wandered off down the hall to the back door, holding the dry creature up to his face and murmuring to it. He said out loud, 'Take this message to the Queen of the Cicadas!' and opened his hand: away it soared into the blue evening. He had forgotten Jenny, imagining that she had gone back to her unpacking, but when he turned he saw that she had followed him softly into the kitchen and was watching him. He laughed uncertainly, caught out in his game, afraid of being thought foolish. He stood poised in the doorway waiting for judgment. She did not know if she could speak.

'I love you,' she whispered.

'Do you?' The light was behind him and she could not see his face. 'I hope so. I want you to.'

At the moment where day passed into night, the house and yard were still.

'You remind me of a lizard,' she said, blushing. 'You remind me of a lizard on a tree trunk.'

He laughed. 'Pommy. I bet you've never even seen a lizard, let alone one on a tree trunk.'

'I have so. I saw it on television.'

'Come here,' he said.

They sat on the step and she put her head on his knee.

'Let me smell your neck,' he said. 'Mmmm. Sweet as a nut. A nut-brown maiden.'

'Do you think we should make a meal?'

'Sooner or later. Hey. Kath and I were a bit hard to take today, weren't we. Talking about old times.'

'It was worse when you were outside and she formally surrendered the crockery and furniture to me. She reminded me of the mother of a bloke I used to live with in England. "Jen–nee! You *do* know how to defrost a fridge, don't you?" She was the closest I ever came to having a real Jewish mother-in-law. She was so generous I kept thinking, "Look out—there's something else going on here."'

They laughed.

'Well,' said Jenny, 'maybe I'll be able to talk with Kath one day, just the two of us.'

'What for? You'll find out what's wrong with me soon enough.'

'No. Not for that.' She sat up and pushed her back into his shoulder. There was still a faint slick of sweat between their skins. 'It's risky, isn't it, what we're doing.'

'Yes. Very.'

'And not very fashionable, either.'

'No. There are quite a few people around who wouldn't mind seeing me slip on a banana peel.'

'Not Kathleen.'

'No. I mean the opinion-makers. The anti-marriage lobby. Of which I remain one of the founding members, as if anyone needed another contradiction.' He let out his sharp, cackling laugh. 'I'm game, if you are.'

She thought she was probably game. She twisted herself round to smile at him. Her teeth were white and good, with a gap between the front two.

'Your teeth are like Terry Thomas's,' he said. 'I saw him once, walking along Exhibition Street. He was wearing a loud check suit. And he said to me, "Hel–lo! Would you laike to go for a raide in mai spawts car?"'

'He did *not*!'

'Actually it was Kath who saw him, not me. Is there any beer left?'

They stepped up into the kitchen and began rummaging for food.

*

They were waiting for Frank.

Flo's half of the children's room was quite bare, once they had put things in piles and packed up her belongings to go. She had few clothes but dozens of books. The room echoed. They stood by the stripped bed, not sure what to do next.

'Want to draw?' said Flo.

They settled down at the table with the box of Derwents between them and coloured away companionably, discussing patterns and the condition of the pencils.

'Gee I'll miss you,' said Kathleen. 'I'll miss that awful piercing voice going "Kath? Kath!"'

'And I'll miss you going "Psst—psst—hurry up!"' said Flo.

They smiled at each other and got on with their work.

'Kathleen,' said Flo after a while. 'Have I got perfect teeth?'

'Who has.'

'Some people do.'

'Mmmm.'

'Kath. Is there anything…sort of…*special* about me?'

'Yes. You've got a wart on your elbow.'

'No! Really.'

'I don't know, Floss. Lots of things, probably.'

'Will you tell me the true answer, if I ask you a serious question?'

'Sure.'

'Am I adopted?'

'Not exactly. I found you under a cabbage.'

Flo drummed her feet, trying not to laugh. 'You said you'd be serious. Am I?'

'No, sweetheart.'

'How can I be sure?'

'*I'm* sure, for God's sake! I lugged you round inside me for nine months, and I had you in the Queen Victoria Hospital, with several witnesses present.'

'Did I hurt, coming out?'

'Yes…but it's not like ordinary pain. You got a bit stuck, after trying to come out for about twenty-six hours. The doctor had to help you out with a thing called forceps, like big tweezers.'

'Yow.' Flo had heard this story at least fifteen times before, and never tired of it. 'What did I look like? Was I cute?'

'It was hard to tell. You were a bit bloody.'

'*Bloody?*'

'There was blood on you.'

'*How come?*'

'Inside the uterus there's lots of spongy stuff partly made out of blood, which you lived in for nine months. And they had to make a little cut in the back of my cunt, to make it bigger and let you out.'

'*Poor Kath*,' said Flo luxuriously.

'Oh no—that part didn't hurt, because they gave me an injection. And then they cut the cord and washed you and wrapped you up in a cotton blanket and let me hold you.'

'Aaaah,' said Flo with her head on one side.

'And then I cried with happiness.'

'Aaaah.' Flo dropped her pencil and came round the table. She backed up to Kathleen and sat on her knee. 'I love that story. It's my favourite story.'

'I'm pretty keen on it too.'

'Guess what—Jenny might be going to have a baby.'

'What?'

'Hey—I can hear a car.' She sprang off her mother's knee and went racing out into the hall. Very carefully Kathleen began to slide the pencils back into their right places.

Kathleen stood outside the front gate with a forgotten jumper in her hands. In the oblong back window of the diminishing car she saw a brown blob become white: Flo turning to look back. A child would be born to which Frank would be father, Flo half-sister, and Kathleen nothing at all. With a sharp gesture she shoved her hands down the little knitted sleeves.

*

Jenny and Frank hardly slept, for days, in their house. He lay with his arm under her neck and round her chest so she was folded neatly with her back against his wiry flank, her right cheek resting on his upper arm.

'Tell me, tell me,' he said.

51

Stumbling at first, finding a pace, she talked to him about her childhood. He asked and asked for details: what sorts of trees? what did you look like? what was on the table? and while she talked he saw again, richly, his own small town, Drought Street, the oval behind the house, the white tank on its stand beside the school, the dusty road, the dry bare leafy dirt of the track home.

'In our marsh there were snipe,' she said.

'We ate monkey nuts,' he replied.

'I sat under a tree, in a striped dress of silky material.'

'A boy had his mouth washed out with soap for swearing.'

'My father had the best garden in the village: people passing in buses admired it over the hedge.'

'I ran a sharp pencil down the big river systems on a plastic template of Australia.'

'My grandmother took me to London for tea. A long white curtain puffed in the wind on to our table: when it fell back there was jam and cream on it.'

'On the first day of school it was so hot that the door of the general store was shut because of the north wind and the dust. I went to buy an exercise book off Mrs Skinner and I sat on the doorstep waiting.'

'My father did his accounts at night, and light came through a hole in the wall up near the ceiling, into my room.'

52

'On the track between the ti-tree the air ticked, and there was a smell like pepper.'

'Were you happy?'

'I don't remember.'

'I don't remember.'

Sleep, what was it? Sometimes Flo stirred or cried out. Someone next door was awake, a white night; they heard soft footsteps, a door closing quietly, a restless person moving. There were hours, it seemed, of lying perfectly still, wide awake, flooded into stillness by the melting of their skins. Secretly, each of them dreamed that Flo was their common child, that they were lying close to each other in some inexpressible dark intimacy of bodies and of history.

After dinner Jenny set herself up with her exercise books at the kitchen table. Flo edged in with a red tartan shirt in her hand.

'Jenny. Is it you who mends my stuff now?'

'Me or Frank. I expect. What is it?'

'I ripped it on the equipment at school. I could ring up Kathleen,' said Flo.

'Um—no, don't do that. Go and hop into bed. You can read till nine o'clock.' How briskly should she speak? Her voice rang falsely in her ears.

'Kath always lets me read till about ten o'clock. Five to ten,' said Flo, speaking rapidly and keeping her eyes on the ground.

'*Flo.*'

'Well, she did! Sometimes!' Flo turned up her face defiantly and went very red; her gaze sheered somewhere to the right of Jenny's. Jenny blushed too.

'Give me the shirt, Flo.'

Flo shoved it at her, darted into her room and sprang into bed. She began to read immediately so as not to think of her failed manoeuvre. Jenny was not sure whether she should go in and kiss her goodnight. She dropped the shirt on to the kitchen table and started twisting a handful of her hair, flicking the springy ends between her fingers and letting her eyes blur. Frank would never notice the tear in the shirt. She could do it quickly now without saying anything, thus adding a drop to the subterranean reservoir of resentment that all women bear towards the men they live with, particularly the ones they love; or she could point it out to him in a *pleasant tone* and they could discuss it like *civilised people*. Why did they always have to be bloody trained? She stuck a piece of hair in the corner of her mouth. She heard the front door slam, and sat down quickly at the table. He came in whistling with eyes bright from the street.

'Frank. There's a problem.'

'What?' He stopped.

'There's a tear in your daughter's shirt.' She pointed at the red garment on the table.

'Oh!' He picked it up by its collar. 'Is it my job, then?'

'I think so.' She was solemn as a judge at the head of the table. 'Also, I've got some other work to do.'

'I can do buttons,' he said doubtfully, 'but I've never been too hot on actual tears.'

She said nothing, hooked her bare feet on the chair rung and fought the treacherous womanly urge. He darted her a quick sideways glance.

'Well!' he said with a rush of his determined cheerfulness. 'I'll see what sort of a fist I can make of it.' He hurried out of the room and returned with an old tea-tin which disgorged a tangled mass of cotton, buttons, coins and drawing pins. Jenny turned back to her books and began to mark them, looking at him every now and then. Frank leaped to the task. He spread the patch over the rip, fidgeted it this way and that, clicked his tongue at his clumsy fingers.

'There! Got the bugger covered. Now for the pins. Heh heh. Just a matter of applying my university education, in the final analysis.'

He looked up. Pen poised, she was gazing at him in that state of voluptuous contemplation with which we watch others at work. With joy he sank the needle into the cloth.

'At the school I went to,' said Jenny in a little while, 'we had an hour of sewing every day. One person read out loud, and the others sewed. We even had to use thimbles.'

'Sounds like *Little Women*,' said Frank, negotiating a corner with his tongue between his teeth. He was sewing away quite competently now. 'Didn't kids muck around?'

'No. It was very peaceful, actually. We all wanted to be nuns for that hour.' She laughed.

'I'm glad it was only an hour a day, then. Otherwise we might never have met. Well—aren't you going to read to me?'

'What shall I read?'

'I'm not fussy.' He was round the corner and on to the home stretch.

She opened a book at random and read, '*Her Anxiety*. Earth in beauty dressed / Awaits returning spring / All true love must die / Alter at the best / Into some lesser thing / Prove that I lie.'

Frank, paying no attention, was holding out the small garment to show her. He was as pleased as Punch.

*

In her room, for days, Kathleen found traces of Flo everywhere: half-filled exercise books, a slice of canteloupe skin with teeth marks along its edges, a skipping rope with wooden handles. She picked up her nightdress and Flo's little flowery one dropped out of its folds.

She wandered out to the kitchen and sat at the table

cutting her fingernails. She sat sideways on her chair looking out the windows at the very clear air. A gum tree over the fence flashed its metallic leaf-backs in the wind. A bird flew across the yard in patchy sunshine, its wings gathered as it coasted on air; it disappeared behind the bamboo which was being jostled by the wind. Kathleen's eyes filled with tears.

'I feel unstable,' she said. 'Not *bad*—just—' She made her flat hand roll like a boat. The other woman at the table looked up over her glasses and nodded, saying nothing.

She worked, throwing away page after page and plugging on, sharpening the pencil every five minutes. The floor around her was sprinkled with shavings. At three thirty she knew it was no good. For four years she had been programmed to stop thinking at school home-time, and will was powerless against this habit. She got under the eiderdown with the most boring book she could find and tried to read herself into a doze so she could get through the moment when Flo would not push open the door and stand there grinning with her schoolbag askew upon her back. In a little while she got up and sat at the table again and kept forcing.

She went for a walk up to the top of the street to the old people's settlement. There were yellow leaves everywhere. She leaned against a gate-post, dull, feeling nothing in particular. An old woman came out her back door to empty a rubbish bin and saw her standing there.

'Hullo dear,' she called. She had a silver perm and knobbly black shoes and an apron which lifted a little in the wind.

'Hullo.'

The woman moved closer. 'Anything wrong?'

'Not really. I'm missing my little girl.'

'Oh.' The old woman knew what she was talking about. Kathleen wanted to ask her the imponderables: what do you understand that I don't? Does it get easier or harder? If she had dared she would have asked something simpler: will you invite me into your kitchen and let me watch you make a cup of tea?

'Do you do any gardening, dear?'

'No.'

'I've found that a great help,' said the old lady. 'My gardens have got me through two nervous breakdowns.'

The old woman was small and wrinkled, and her large earlobes had become floppy with the weight of the gold rings that hung from them. Her skin looked waxy, and on her cheekbones were several enormous blackheads. Her dark blue crepe dress, unlike Kathleen's, had probably been owned by the same person ever since it was bought. She was not looking at Kathleen, perhaps so as to spare her from social duty, but simply stood beside her, following her gaze to the turbulence of coloured clouds behind the trees in their fullness, the upper sky veiled with pale grey, the parsley trembling in thin rows, the worn-out tea towels showing their warp and woof on the line. In a little while she heaved a sigh, and gave Kathleen a quick look from her bright eyes. 'Well. Back to work, I s'pose. It'll be teatime d'rectly. Ta ta!'

'Bye,' said Kathleen, and walked on.

Flo's voice sounded very high-pitched and childish on the phone.

'How's everything over there, Flo?'

'Oh, great! We have roast pork, and Jenny makes these great noodles.'

'Are you getting to school OK?'

'Well...' She gave an adventurous giggle. 'Frank said not to *say* but most mornings I'm late, because Frank and Jenny don't wake up as early as you do.'

What mean satisfaction she derived from this. 'I bet you drag the chain, do you?'

'A bit.'

A pause fell. Flo was making crunching noises.

'What are you eating?'

'A carrot.'

Kathleen felt shy and importunate. She had no small talk.

'Kath? Know what I wish?'

'What.'

'I wish we could all live together.'

'Who?'

'You, and me, and Jenny, and Frank.'

'Hmm. I'm afraid that's almost certainly never going to happen.'

'But *why*?'

'There's not a room for me over there, for a start.'

'You could sleep in my room, with me.'

'I don't think so. I don't think I'd be very... welcome.'

'I *wish* you could!' cried Flo urgently, as if mere force of desire might change a hostile destiny.

'I could come and live in the broom cupboard, and every time Jenny or Frank opened it I'd pop out and sing that song that goes, "Ullo! I'm a reject / Does one arm 'ang down longer?"'

'Don't talk like that, Kath.' Flo's voice was heavy with disapproval. 'You're trying to make me not like Jenny.'

'Excuse me,' said Kathleen, mortified at her own grossness. 'What a nasty thing to say. And not even historically correct.'

'Never mind. I didn't think you really meant it. When are you coming to visit? So you and I can cook, and have the meal ready to surprise Frank and Jenny?'

'I could come on Tuesday. You go and ask Frank now if that's all right.'

Flo muffled the phone with her hand. Tuesday was all right. There was nothing else to say so they hung up.

60

Before Tuesday could come, the old man died. He stepped out of the bath and his heart simply stopped.

The ground they stood on was untended, unlawned, littered untidily with fallen gum leaves and unruly twigs. The trees gave no sign of autumn in the bush cemetery, but it was in the light, its doubtful angle, its mildness on the skin. Shirley's eye rolled on that strange warm day but she gave Flo a thick bunch of roses to hold in her two fists beside the grave. Beside the grave in order stood: Shirley, trembling and smiling into space like a vague hostess; Frank, frowning and clearing his throat and standing with his heels together and daylight between his knees; Flo, wishing the coffin lid might open a crack so she could see a dead body; Kathleen, folding herself, putting herself away now, decorous as a spectre; Jenny, almost wife but fighting it, singed from behind by the inquisitiveness of Frank's cousins and (to Frank, who saw how her brown smooth skin made her lips seem pinker) suddenly resembling Flo, as all people we love at moments resemble each other.

At the house people laughed more than they had thought they would, or ought to. Against a clock stood a very old photograph of Jack as a boy in a striped suit with short pants and lace-up boots; his face bore the good-natured, musing expression he had never lost.

'It's a beautiful photo, Mrs Maxwell,' said Jenny.

'I'll bet he hated that suit!' cried Shirley with the shrill laugh of someone right on the edge.

'Poor Papa,' agonised Flo, who wanted there to be more tragedy in the occasion. 'He was a good man, wasn't he, Nanna. He led a good life.'

'He certainly did, sweetheart. Oh, he was the kindest of men.'

Shirley seized Flo in her skinny arms and they hugged eagerly, their eyes full of tears. 'The first time he asked me out,' she went on in a conspiratorial tone, glancing around her as she spoke, 'we drove out into the country. There we sat among the bush irises— flags, we used to call them—white and blue—and Jack asked me if I wanted a drink!' Her laugh cracked in the middle. 'He must've thought I drank! Well, I did, I suppose—and he said he had a bottle of beer in the car. I thought, Oh good, this is nice. And he got the bottle out of the car but he didn't have an opener because *he* didn't drink! So he knocked the top off the bottle against a tree. And I've often thought, later, we could've died. One piece of broken glass.'

Over by the window, behind the couch on which the three women and the child were sitting, one of the cousins was hissing to Frank.

'Who's the new one, Frankie? Got any legal advice?'

Frank tossed his empty glass from palm to palm, smiling furiously and whistling through his teeth.

'We're all *reasonable people*, Brian,' he replied in a light, tense voice.

'Ah yeah...that's what they all say.' The cousin laughed loosely and looked away. He planted his feet wide apart and tightened his thighs like a footballer. 'You'll end up paying a packet in alimony, mate,' he predicted comfortably, draining his glass.

Shirley, Jenny and Kathleen walked down to the beach in their funeral clothes. Their heels sank and they sat down in the sand, Shirley in the middle, and watched the water, the oceanward rushing of the tide, the tiny waves crisping helplessly towards the leftover line of dried seaweed that ran crookedly all along the water's edge. The younger women, set about the older one like a pair of brackets, did not know each other, did not know what they were protecting the mother-in-law from, but felt their positions to be proper.

'What am I going to do now?' asked Shirley.

Nobody answered. The sea ran by. The day seemed very long to them all.

*

Flo dangled maddeningly over into the front seat and whistled and called to the dog. 'Come! Come! Come in the back with me!'

63

'Don't treat the dog like a toy, Flo,' said Jenny, irritated. 'She wants to stay in the front with me.'

'It's all right for you two!' burst out Flo, flinging herself back into her seat. 'There's plenty of love in the front seat, but none in the back.'

'Are you jealous?' said Frank. He winked at her over his shoulder.

'*I am not jealous*,' cried Flo in a fury. She slouched in her corner and stared out at the trees. 'I haven't got anything to *do*.'

'We told you if you came away with us there'd be no whingeing,' said Frank.

'I am *not whingeing*.'

'Look out the window, then.'

'There's nothing to *see*.'

Jenny glanced back over her shoulder and caught an odd cast to Flo's scowling face: a snubbing of nose, a stretching of eyes, a rising of top lip. She looked sinister. The word passed instantly and was forgotten.

The wind tore steadily past the house, racing off the sea and over the sandhills and up the gravelly drive and through the scraggy hedge. All day the house groaned and shook in the wind, which relented a little at nightfall, leaving pinkish clouds looped neatly above the drab green humps of ti-tree. They were all sunburned in such a way that the sides of their fingers looked silvery-white, as if they were underwater.

On the clifftop the wind still blustered fitfully. On the ocean beach they made a fire, and Frank and Flo ran half a mile beside the cold white and green surf, still clear to Jenny's eyes no matter how far they ran, so empty was the air. She wrapped herself in a sleeping bag and waited for stars, roasting her face and chilling her back; before it was dark the others came panting back to her through the soft sand. The first planet swung for them, burned pink and green like a prism, spinning idly in the firmament.

The wind blew itself right out in the dark, and next morning sun was flooding quietly into the beach house when they awoke.

Five in the afternoon was the appointed hour, but when Kathleen crossed the creaking verandah and knocked at the front door, the house was silent. No dog barked. She tried the side gate, but it was locked from the inside and had no hand-hole by which she might have climbed it and gone down to the back door. It was quite shocking to her to be locked out of the house of people she knew. She was aggrieved and hurt and cross. It was hot. She sat bad-temperedly on the verandah and swore to herself. Surely they couldn't have forgotten her.

After ten minutes she got up and tried the front window. It slid up obediently. Jubilant, she crawled in, closed it behind her and ran down to the kitchen where she filled the kettle and set about making herself a drink and a snack, the ingredients for which she found in abundance in the fridge. She opened the back door and sat contentedly on the step, chewing and swallowing.

Half an hour later a key rattled in the front door and they were upon her: the dog yapping dutifully, Flo leaping on her back with cries of welcome, Frank looking preoccupied, Jenny frozen-faced and very sharp-footed. At the sight of Jenny, whose eyes avoided hers after the first obligatory greeting, Kathleen realised that something was badly wrong. She scrambled to her feet, noticing that her shirt was covered with crumbs. Jenny opened the fridge and began to forage in the lower shelves.

'There's a fresh pot of tea made,' said Kathleen, performing a dance of appeasement behind Jenny's back. Flo was dragging at her, and she followed into the girl's bedroom.

'What will we make for dinner?' Flo was saying, sitting up importantly at her table. 'We could have a tomato salad, and ice-cream.'

Kathleen knew that everything she said would be overheard in the kitchen, where the silence was being broken only by the movement of feet and chair legs on the wooden floor. She felt miserable, superfluous, and would have disappeared as impolitely as she had come had it not been for oblivious Flo with her pencil and paper, waiting eagerly for her reply.

'Hold your horses, Flo,' she said quietly. 'I don't think we're going to be able to make the dinner after all.'

'But why?'

'Because...' She heard Jenny's heels go out of the kitchen in the other direction. 'Because maybe Jenny or Frank would rather do the cooking here. I'm a guest—guests aren't supposed to act as if they owned the place.'

Flo could see her plans slipping out of her grasp again, sliding away for reasons that would be carefully explained to her in words of one syllable, adding to the load of childish trouble not of her making that she must lug about with her. She let out the eternal cry of childhood, prelude to resignation: 'It's not fair!'

At that moment Frank stepped into the room. He was smiling awkwardly. 'Kath—look, don't get excited—I want to talk to you for a minute. There's a crisis on here.'

Kathleen's face was burning with resentment. She knew what was coming, and stuck out her chin to cop it.

'Now listen—' He was unconsciously making calming movements with his flat hands. 'Jenny's feeling extremely...*uncomfortable* that you're here.'

'But I was invited!' she cried, knowing that by climbing in the window she had effectively dispensed Jenny from the hostly obligations that would have otherwise been due. She sat there on the edge of the bed, spine erect, hands under thighs, feet dangling.

'Yes, yes, I know. But—you didn't—*wait*. You—'

'I know. I came in the window. Well, what am I going to do now? I came to see Flo. That's why I *came*.' Although this was true, she had a nasty feeling that it was not the whole story. She saw that Frank was floundering out of his depth, did not know what was the right thing to do, hated carrying the bad news between the two women who were too cowardly to face each other. She was full of disgust, and pity, for all of them.

'We're going to have to talk about a few things,' said Frank urgently. 'Can you meet me and Flo at the school in the morning? Eight thirty?'

'OK.' She got off the bed.

'You're not going *home*, are you, Kath?' Flo too was in over her head.

'Let's go out in the backyard, Flo, just you and me,' said Kathleen desperately. 'And we'll think what to do.'

They shuffled outside past Frank who nodded anxiously at them, and squatted against the fence at the very bottom of the yard. The little dog nosed about them, and Flo scratched its woolly coat and squinted up at her mother, waiting for enlightenment.

'I made a mistake, Floss. I shouldn't have climbed in the window when there was nobody home.'

'But there's nothing wrong with climbing in some-one's window. We used to always get in the window at Sutherland Street, if we forgot the key, and so did everyone else.' There was a moral in here somewhere, Flo knew, and she wrestled to get at it.

'Yes, but Jenny's never lived like us, in big open houses where groups of people live and anyone can come in and out in the daytime and the night. She doesn't agree with that sort of way of living. Most people would be mad if they invited someone to dinner and came home and found them already making them-selves a snack in the kitchen.' She felt quite giddy and disorientated, trying to remember ordinary social formalities. 'Also,' she went on, forcing herself, 'there are sometimes funny feelings between an old wife and a new one.'

'Jenny isn't Frank's wife. You are.'

'That's true in one way. But Jenny lives with Frank now, and I don't any more, so it's sort of the same, really.'

The little girl squeezed the struggling dog in her arms. 'I don't like this,' she said stubbornly. 'I asked you to come and visit, and nothing's working out like I want it. It's not fair. I don't think grown-ups should fight when children want to have a visitor.'

The back door banged and Jenny, who had taken off her shoes, was coming down the yard towards them with a glass of wine in her hand. She crouched down three feet in front of Kathleen and offered her the glass. The two women looked each other steadily in the eyes, and their mouths curved in identical grimaces of embarrassment which they could neither conceal nor metamorphose into smiles. It was the best they could manage.

Kathleen leaned against the school gate from eight thirty till nine o'clock when the siren cleared the yard of children and only a few papers blew about in the dust. She was wondering whether it was time to panic when she spotted Frank and Flo, walking hand in hand and uncharacteristically slowly, coming round the building from the other side. She rushed up to them.

'Where were you! I've been waiting for half an hour.'

'We said at the *gate*,' said Flo, her face straining against tears. 'We've been at the *gate*, we got there at half past and you weren't *there*.'

'Oh Floss! We were at different gates.' She dropped to her haunches, but the child stood stiffly holding her father's hand, unapproachable.

Frank was darting agitated looks about him. 'Let's get out of here. We could go to the espresso bar.'

Kathleen took Flo's other hand and they crossed the road and sat at the window table of the café, Flo in the middle, one parent at each end. Kathleen began.

'I know I shouldn't have climbed in the window. I'm not in the habit of climbing in windows.' Her voice sounded huffy, and Frank let out an impatient laugh.

'Windows, windows! What we should really be talking about is getting this bloody divorce.'

'*Divorce*'? Flo burst out sobbing. 'Oh no! I don't *want* you to get a divorce!'

'Come and sit on my knee, Floss,' said Kathleen wretchedly.

'No!' She fought them both off and sobbed desperately in the exact middle of her side of the table, refusing to touch either of them, battling for honour.

'But Flo!' said Frank. 'Divorce is no different from how me and Kath have already been living for years!'

'I don't care! Oh, I want us *all* to live together, in the same house. Can't we all go back to Sutherland Street? I *know* it would work! Oh, can't we?'

She wept bitterly, in floods of grief: she did not touch her face, for she was sitting on her hands so that neither of her parents might seize one and sway her into partiality. The tears, unwiped, splashed off her cheeks and on to the table. The Italian waiter behind the espresso machine turned his face away in distress, his hands still clinging to the upright handles.

'It's just—it's just *life*, Flo,' stammered Frank, the tears standing in his eyes. 'We have to make the best we can of it.'

They sat helplessly at the table, survivors of an attempt at a family, while the little girl wept aloud

71

for the three of them, for things that had gone wrong before she was born and when she was only a baby, for the hard truth which they had thought to escape by running parallel with it instead of tackling it head on.

*

By nightfall there was nowhere else to go.

Jenny opened the door in a night-dress, red pencil in hand, curly hair pinned back off her forehead. With her shoes off she was the same height as Kathleen.

'Oh. I was working. Frank's out.'

'It was to see you. Excuse me for coming without being invited.'

'Oh Kathleen. I'm not a monster, you know.'

'Neither am I.'

'Come in.' She stood aside. Flo was curled up on the floor. The book had slipped sideways from her hand, and her mouth was open. A little trail of dribble had wet the cushion. The women sat down on two hard chairs.

'I came because, because things are a bit much for me, right now. I'm a mess, in fact.'

'You, a mess?'

'Do I have to break plates?'

'No. I shall try to see for myself.'

'All this is very painful for me. I can't get used to living without Flo.'

'I thought Frank said you wanted to work.'

'I *do*. But it's so long now that I've had to make my life fit around her—it doesn't make sense without her.' She twisted her face, trying to make a joke. 'I'm bored. I don't get any laughs.'

'I have the impression that you judge the whole tenor of your life by whether or not you're laughing enough.'

'You could say that.'

'I don't know if that's a good criterion.'

'Know any better ones?'

'Why is it so important, laughing?'

'Look. I've got this sign stuck on my bedroom wall. It's by Cocteau. It says, *What would become of me without laughter? It purges me of my disgust.*'

'What disgusts you?'

'Oh, my whole life, sometimes. Things I've done. Things I haven't done. My big mouth. My tone of voice. The gap between theory and practice. The fact that I can't stand to read the paper.'

They looked down uncomfortably.

'Sometimes the only person I can stand is Floss here. For years I've thought I'd be glad to see the back of her. Now I don't know what to do with myself. I roam around. Try to work. Think about falling in love. I can't help thinking of all the horrible things I've done to Flo and Frank.'

'What things?'

There was a long pause.

'I've never told anyone about this.'

'You don't have to.'

'Once, a long time ago, I ran away with another bloke. I was crazy about him. I didn't care about anything else. I felt as if I'd just been born.' She blushed and pushed her clasped hands between her thighs. 'One night, walking along the street, I told him I loved him more than I loved Flo.' She laughed. 'I even thought it was true. Pathetic, isn't it.'

'No.'

'Anyway. I wanted to go away with him. Frank, Frank cried, he got drunk and broke all the windows upstairs, kicked them in. I was so scared I fainted and fell down the stairs. It was the middle of the night. One of the girls downstairs picked me up and dusted me off. Frank was out in the street by that time chucking empty milk bottles around. She said, Frank's being ridiculous. But he wasn't.' She breathed out sharply through her nose. 'I went away with the other bloke. Flo was only about two, at the time. One morning I came back, on my way to work. I walked in the front door and in the lounge room I saw Flo sitting up in front of the television. She must have just woken up. She was all blurry and confused. She didn't see me. She was sitting in an armchair with her feet sticking out, all by herself in the room. It was Sesame Street. And Frank came into the room with a bowl of Corn Flakes for her breakfast. He had this look—his face was—I can't talk about this.' Kathleen put her face on her arms on the back of the chair, lifted it up again, and went on. 'He was trying to get ready for work and feed her and do everything. He was *running*.'

Neither of them spoke.

'I suppose it doesn't sound like much,' said Kathleen.

'Go on. I'm listening.'

'Of course, I was absolutely miserable with this other bloke. I used to type his fucking essays for him. Jesus. He had this way of looking at my clothes. I couldn't do anything right. He told me I was like a bull in the china shop. Of his heart.' Again she tried to laugh. 'I don't know why I'm telling *you* this. There are some things I'll never forgive myself for. That morning I was talking about. Never. I don't know if you…'

Jenny leaned forward and spoke very clearly. 'Listen, Kathleen. I'm nuts about Frank. *Nuts* about him.'

Flo, who had turned over on to her back with her knees splayed like a frog, drew herself together with a start and sat up.

'Oh! I dreamed! Hullo Kath! Did I go to sleep? When are we going?'

'Going where?' said Jenny.

'Down to the park to play on the swings, like you said at tea-time.'

75

'That was hours ago, Floss. It's nearly ten o'clock. And I'm only in my nightie.'

'What if we all went down,' said Kathleen. 'Just for quarter of an hour.'

'I only said that because I thought mothers were supposed to,' said Jenny. 'If I put a belt on, it will look like a dress.'

Outside the gate Flo galloped ahead with the dog. The two women came along slowly in the almost-dark. The sky, which was indigo, had withdrawn to the heights as if to make room for a sliver of moon, dark dusky yellow, rocked on its back like a cradle.

'Kathleen? I don't feel disgusted. Kath? When I met Frank, I knew he liked me, because he kept his body turned towards me all the time, wherever I was in the room. We were in a room with some other people. I didn't know him.'

'Frank and I had a dog, once. But he got a disease. He was going to die. I carried him to the vet wrapped up in an old blue coat. I put him on the table and they were going to give him an injection. We went walking in the Botanic Gardens, after we left him. We were both crying. Then we saw a bird hop in a bush.'

'I dreamed about you and me becoming friends. I've been in Australia two years now, and I haven't got a good girlfriend.'

'But I was unbearable, the day we moved the furniture, and climbing in the window.'

'You were always barging on to my territory.'

In the park, beside the concrete wall of the football ground, the women sat down close together on the shaven grass. There was a strong scent of gums, and earth.

'Are you having a baby? Flo told me you might be.'

'I thought I was pregnant, but not yet. I'm going to. I want to.'

Flo and the dog were tearing about in the thickening darkness, over by the swings and slides. They saw her leap up and grab the high end of the see-saw.

'Hey! Come over here! Jenny? Kath? Come over!' She was beckoning enthusiastically.

They got up and picked their way barefoot off the grass and across the lumpy gravel.

'It's a game,' said Flo. 'You two get on.'

They hesitated, glanced at each other and away again. Flo was nodding and smiling and raising her eyebrows, one hand holding the ridged wooden plank horizontal. They separated and walked away from each other, one to each end. They swung their legs over and placed themselves gingerly, easing their weight this way and that on the meandering board.

'Let go, Floss.'

The child stepped back. Jenny, who was nearer the ground, gave a firm shove with one foot to send the plank into motion. It responded. It rose without haste, sweetly, to the level, steadied, and stopped.

They hung in the dark, airily balancing, motionless.

77

Other People's Children

Madigan was a great lump of a fellow with yellow eyes, who bunched his thick fingers together in front of him when he entered a room, and walked with legs that seemed too heavy for the top of his body. His eyes bulged behind warped plastic-rimmed spectacles; his eye-lashes pressed against the lenses. Kin to Madigan were autodidacts who transcribed reams from reference books in public libraries, sniffing and murmuring and grinding their teeth, wearing huge black vinyl gloves as they pushed the biro.

He lived with some hippies in a cavernous, ivy-covered house south of the Yarra. His room was a converted shed that sagged against the back fence. Madigan hid in there. Sometimes he would grit his teeth and go inside for a couple of hours to the kitchen where the others sat round the table under the hanging light bulb rolling joints and drinking Formosan tea, talking about massage and colonic irrigation, agreeing with each other, complaining soothingly in soft voices. He secretly despised the way their voices went up at the end of each sentence, as if they waited for approval before continuing. When they talked, when they sighed 'Ama–a–azing!' he felt like a fox living in a chicken coop. But he needed them, for company, for human presence near him in the chilly house, and to buy food and cook it; and because without them he wouldn't have had a room at all and would have had to offer himself to some soft-hearted feminist who would give him a roof and a side of the bed in exchange for his helplessness and the occasional surprise of his cutting humour.

They were kind people, though; vague, and years younger than he was. They patronised him and deferred to him and discussed him behind his back.

'Madigan's pretty well unemployable?' they reassured each other. 'He'll probably never get his shit together?'

The women worked at odd things, tolerated the three children of one of them, cooked huge, ill-assorted vegetarian meals, and listened respectfully to the opinions of the men, all of whom were musicians of one stripe or another. If the men wanted meat, they had to go round the corner to the Greek's.

Every second Tuesday Madigan dressed himself neatly, combed his colourless hair, and strolled to the dole office. When he got his cheque, he handed over to Myra his share of the rent and food money as faithfully as a good husband on payday.

Madigan sat outside the State Library at lunch time, watching for normal life. His anxious nature, knotted as a mallee root with scruple and doubt, yearned towards a grey-haired man of fifty on a bench who bent earnestly over the hand of a woman, clasped her fingers with earnestness, leaned forward over their clasped fingers; all the while seagulls jostled rudely round their ankles, keeping up a chorus of ill-tempered cries and squawks. The woman stared straight ahead in her yellow cardigan, her mouth closed over false teeth, her feet in cheap sandals balancing stiffly on their heels, her toes pointing upwards at a forty-five degree angle. Was the man saying 'Come back to me'? What had the man done, that she would not look at him on this public bench? Madigan turned away discreetly.

He mooned round milk bar windows looking for hand-lettered signs. He dreamed up small agonies over *Wanted: one kitten preferably fluffy please call at number 5 Park Street* and *Mrs Day wanted: canary whistler will give good home*. He passed the pubs in Gertrude Street and heard them, through the open door, singing *Cuando cuando cuando cuando*.

In the Eye Hospital Out-patients, the hooks of other people's conversations lodged themselves among his nerves.

'Cor,' croaked a woman opposite him, noticing a mistake in her knitting. 'Right in the flamin' neck.'

'What's that woman?' said her friend.

'Vietnamese?'

'Japanese.'

'Could be Malay.'

'No. Can't be Malay. She hasn't got the hair. Malays have got curly hair.'

'See that girl over there who needed an interpreter? Well I think she's from Italy. 'Cause she's got Italy written on her bag.'

Madigan was from a town on the south coast of Queensland and he wished he could go back, he longed to go back, but he had to stay now, might as well, because he had lugged all his stuff down and was thinking of unpacking it, and because Margaret had finally been driven off the edge by his dithering, and because he was a professional, and he was going to work, though nobody down here had heard of him yet.

The last time he went up north to visit his parents, he hitched, carrying the harmonicas in an old cotton pillowcase. A fat, stupid couple picked him up. They stopped for petrol somewhere in the middle of a starry night. Madigan, thinking to be a guest, stepped out into the thick warm air, crossed to the roadhouse and bought three cans of drink. He went to the window of the car and offered a can to the man, who gave him a suspicious stare and shook his head. Madigan put the cans in his bag and returned to the back seat. The fat, stupid man screwed himself round to speak over the seat.

'Funny thing happened,' said the man. 'Bloke just come up to me window and asked me if I wanted a tin of drink.'

Madigan's mother was squat, bow-legged, fearful, dim. She believed that everything wrong in the world was due to the influence of some cult or other. His father worked for the local council. Madigan borrowed twenty dollars from his mother one morning after his father had left for work, and wandered up to the main street, carrying his harps and wondering if he had the stamina to busk. He went into an espresso bar to think about it and sat down at the table next to the tinted window, with the twenty dollars in his pocket. As the cappuccino popped its creamy bubbles pleasantly before him, a rhythmic movement low down on the footpath outside the window caught his eye. He glanced down and saw his father crawl past on his hands and knees. He was smoothing out fresh concrete.

Drinking coffee made Madigan nervous, anyway.

He was back in Melbourne for the next dole day. They gave him a job, which he accepted willingly, washing dishes in a restaurant. He told the others at home that he was pearl-diving, giving it a weary professional ring. They laughed fondly. Myra imagined him standing at the sink in his dream, up to the elbows

85

in greasy water, the shrill thunder of the restaurant kitchen battering round his ears. He wouldn't last three days in a job where you had to work fast. She leaned across the table to give his arm an affectionate press. He saw the hand coming, the fingers stained green by cheap copper rings, and jerked back out of her reach with a look of panic, then tried to transform his reaction into a suave movement towards the teapot. He thought Myra was probably on the look-out for a man in her life, a responsible chap, someone to look after the kids. Or maybe she even wanted to fuck him. Oh God. He bolted out the back and into his shed and under the eiderdown. His hands were all wrinkly and ridged from the hot water. Maybe he should buy some rubber gloves. He could think about that tomorrow.

*

In another kitchen four or five miles up the Punt Road bus route, a match scratched and the little flower of gas blossomed. It was six thirty in the morning. No one would have been fool enough to address Scotty before the first coffee had coursed in her bloodstream. She stood sternly at the stove in her loose pyjamas and waited for the kettle. She rolled out the griller and saw mouse-marks in the chop fat; on the bench ants thronged round an open jam jar. She clicked her tongue, lowered her imposing brow, and massacred the ants with a hot, wrung-out dish-cloth. Then she seized a red texta and a sheet of butcher paper from the table drawer and wrote in a smooth teacher's script:

I wish people who were 'into' midnight 'munchies' would develop an ant *and* mouse *'consciousness'.*

She sticky-taped the notice to the glass of the back door so that everyone would see it on their way out to the lavatory, and stepped out on to the bricks. There was a small bony moon very high up in a clear sky. The sun itself was not yet visible but was casting a pink light on to the underside of leaves. She planted her feet in the grass, rolled the pyjama pants up to her knees, and began to bend and stretch. She was a straight-backed, dark-haired girl with firm flesh on her and plenty of it. Her feet were high-arched, her ankles hollow. She thought she was too fat, but she was flexible as she bent this way and that, her movements severely graceful. Her round face, which fell habitually into a disgruntled expression, smoothed itself with concentration. Sweat began to gleam on her broad forehead.

Someone came out the door behind her. Scotty stopped, doubled over with her legs wide apart and her head hanging between her knees. It was Ruth, with a guilty expression and a white china potty in one hand, heading for the lavatory. She hurried past.

Water rushed in the wooden stall and she emerged.

'I know I should walk out to the dunny at night, like you do, Scotty,' she called, risking it.

'Oh, don't defer to me, Ruth. I make myself sick. I'm such a fucking puritan.' Scotty straightened up, flushing. 'I hate those meetings. They're just fights with somebody taking notes.'

Ruth came across the grass, her smooth, Irish-jawed face confused with sleep and troublesome thoughts, her thatch of reddish hair standing on end. They looked at each other for a moment, without expression.

'I'm sorry, Ruth,' said Scotty.

'So am I. I get that wild with you I don't know what I'm saying.'

'I hate it when we fight. Specially about the kids.'

'So do I,' said Ruth. 'I heard you go out the door last night. I started wondering if there's something about me that makes people go out in a rage and slam the door. Jim was always doing it.'

'I was miserable.'

'Miserable? I thought you were just mad, and sick of me.'

'Of course I was miserable! Look at my tongue—it's covered in ulcers! Jesus, Ruth—what do you think I *am*?'

Ruth looked down at her bony feet in the grass. 'Sometimes I wonder what you're feelin'. Or even *if* you're feelin'. You're always so rational. You've got the gift of the gab. I can't keep up.'

'I've been *trained* to have the gift of the gab,' said Scotty, 'and that's what you liked about me at the beginning. You thought because I could talk I must know more than you. And so you wanted me to tell you what to do—be your mother, a bit. And now you see I'm just ordinary—got feet of clay—you sort of can't forgive me.'

In Ruth's eyes shone a beam of dogged loyalty to old friendship. 'I got nothin' against clay,' she said. 'It's what our plates are made of—what we eat off every day.'

Scotty laughed. 'You should write songs.'

The sky rippled with smooth bars of pink and gold. People were stirring inside the house. A door slammed, a child's voice was raised in anger, or mirth.

'The lines aren't drawn yet, are they, Scotty?'

'I hope not.'

'What if we blow it?'

'I dunno.'

'Here, Scott. Give us a hug.'

They were dissolved. Ruth was tall enough for Scotty's head to lie on her shoulder. Such hopes they had had! It was a moment of grace, beyond will or reason, and might never be repeated. They let go.

'Where'd you go?' said Ruth.

'Oh, I ended up at Alex's gig,' said Scotty. She recommended the exercises and her voice came and went among her limbs, punctuated with sharp expulsions of breath. 'I met this guy.'

'Oo, hoo! Did you go home with him?'

'*Hang* on! I met this guy, who Alex knew, and we had a drink, and after the gig we drove him home, and he was weird.'

'You didn't go home with him then?'

'I didn't get out of the car. Thank goodness.'

'Aaaah.' Ruth was disappointed. She was a one-man woman, and when she went out it was to visit friends in familiar houses, or to talk politics in pubs, or to meetings, not to dance and drink too much whisky and stagger home with strangers.

'I'm not a hooer, you know.' Scotty stood up at last, her cheeks shining and damp. 'I'm not a band moll.'

'I didn't mean *that*,' said Ruth hastily.

A raffish grey dog bounded into the kitchen, followed by a girl in a pink dressing-gown. The dressing-gown cord was tied in a neat bow round her portly little torso. She had thousands of freckles and the pale, blinking countenance of the bespectacled. Her large feet were shod in pink slippers with pompoms; and she had tried to flatten the waves of her hair with a series of bobby-pins crossed at strategic points. Something matronly about her, at eight years old, pierced grown-ups' hearts, but her eyes were watchful with the plain child's pride. She went straight to a chair and sat holding the dog's head between her knees and picking the crusty sleep out of the corners of its eyes.

'Good morning, Laurel,' said Scotty.

Laurel looked up. 'Polly's silly,' she remarked. 'You give her a b-a-l-l and she chews it to bits. You give her a b-o-n-e and she just buries it.'

'What's a b-o-n?' said a thick voice at the door.

'Bone, Wally, you idiot,' cried Laurel in sudden rage.

'Don't call your brother an idiot,' said Ruth.

'Yeah. Shut your face, fatty,' said the boy. 'Come on, Poll.' He clapped his hands in front of the dog and it began to leap off the ground as high as his shoulder. At the height of each leap it seemed to hang for a second in mid-air, ears flying, legs dangling, like a jelly-fish in deep water. It emitted sharp yips.

'Get the dog outside,' said Scotty, in the level voice of someone accustomed to being obeyed.

Wally looked up resentfully, but he had felt the flat of Scotty's hand before when his mother was not about, so he ushered the dog out and slammed the screen door behind it.

Whenever Ruth washed herself with Johnson's baby soap, she remembered when Laurel was a baby. They lived in a tall, dark terrace house with a yard full of useless sheds, behind which, when they moved in, she had found stuffed dozens of blood-soaked sanitary

91

pads, dry and crackly and blackened. In the kitchen were two old troughs. She brought hot water in from the bathroom in a plastic bucket. The floor was of brick. Once the dog had surprised a rat among the paper bags in the cupboard under the sink: the dog bristled and roared, Ruth screamed, the rat thrashed about among the bags (they could only hear it) and shot suddenly into view through a crack, up the wall and out through a gap in the timber round an ill-fitted pipe.

With the Johnson's baby soap she ran her slippery hands gently over Laurel's solid body; the water in the plastic tub lapped sweetly, her hands slid and met no resistance; the baby's head lolled in her palm, her hands moved effortlessly at the child's flesh.

Jim was never there, except for dinner when he would cheerfully ram food into his large mouth, kiss her and dash off out the front door. He came home at four in the morning smelling of beer and sometimes perfume. He had crowds of friends at university. He told her he had set himself up at a table in the union building behind a sign saying *Any questions answered 20 cents*. He sat eagerly, cross-legged, talking, talking, talking. He even stole from her her own stories: once she had woken in the night, feeling something was wrong; she ran into the baby's room and found Laurel sitting up in the cot, clinging to the bars and staring at the overturned radiator which had already burned its way right through the matting and one layer of lino—flames were starting to lick up round it. Bullshit, he said with a laugh. There weren't any flames! And I got there first. There was only a lot of smoke and you panicked. He never told her she was stupid in so many words, but she felt he thought so, and she became stupid, frightened of words of more than one syllable, thick-thoughted, easily confused by anyone with a ready tongue.

They never went anywhere, never went out into the country looking for firewood or mushrooms, never went drinking together in pubs, for he was always in company and none of them liked her. Once he shat his pants from laughing. He swaggered in bow-legged, still grinning, and dropped the stained jeans and under-pants on the bathroom floor for her to wash them. Once, when she cried about her life, stuck there in the house with Laurel and the dog, he had taken her with him to the pub. She slid herself behind the long table, and the talking faces swung towards her for a second, summed her up and—worse than dismissed—smiled blankly. She knew one of the women from her own cut-short university days. The woman nodded to her. Ruth drank in silence, holding the baby on her lap, as the voices shrieked around her. Some of them were doing a play and seemed to be conversing in lines from the script, which made no sense to her but set the others roaring. One of the men, in a pause in the talk, raised his glass and stared at Ruth and said in a loud, hearty voice,

'I see some of us have brought their wives with them tonight. Let's hear it for 'em' and farted with his pursed lips. No one said anything. Then Jim sprang to his feet and seized the man's collar in mock rage.

'Come on—let's step outside,' he said. The man laughed and they exchanged joking cuffs to the ear, then sank back into their places, honour satisfied. The volume of sound swelled again and Ruth was forgotten. She sat with flaming cheeks, and blushed and blushed until the backs of her eyes sang.

When Jim woke up, it was too late. She didn't love him any more. She didn't love anyone. She had the other child and breast-fed him in a dream; she weaned him and washed the milk off the front of her clothes and lost two stone and sat all day in one of the downstairs rooms reading pamphlets. Now it was her turn to be out all the time. She was mean, he said. She said, 'If you're not here to take the kids on the dot of ten tomorrow you won't be seeing them again.' He danced about in a kind of hysterical sulking. She stood unmoved by the door. He saw she meant it. He was there on the dot of ten, but she wasn't. She was round the corner at a friend's place, waiting for ten fifteen before she came home. If there was one thing Ruth understood, it was the power of absence. Away he went in the old Holden with Wally asleep in his basket on the back seat and Laurel waving out the side window. When they weren't there she didn't know what to do with herself. She wandered round the city in darned clothes that hung off her, staring at herself in windows. In a big shop full of silky dresses she heard a man singing in a high-pitched, yearning voice, which entered unobstructed into her hollow head,

'*Helpless, helpless, help–less…*'

She didn't think about the words, but tears ran down her face.

She told Jim to go. He cried,

'But I still love you. What am I going to do with the love?'

It was a word that neither of them had yet learned the meaning of.

She was quite calm inside, watching him writhe flat on his face on the bed. Hadn't he ever cried before? His sobs were like vomiting, so hard was it for him to bring up grief.

'It's too late, Jimmy,' she said. 'I'm sorry I'm hurting you, but it's too late.'

'You're not keeping *both* the kids, are you? *Oh*,' he wept. 'Let me take Wally.' He sat up and wiped his eyes. Wrinkles she had never noticed before fanned out from his eyes, cut like brackets round his mouth. 'I promise, I promise I'll look after him. I couldn't bear it if you kept them both.'

95

Laurel was the one she had been lost in, lost with. While Ruth had roamed the empty rooms, unreachable, Laurel had plodded after her; once, while Ruth raged to herself, Laurel had punched herself in the head with a dull rhythm. They were bound together in that history. Jim took Wally, who was still not much more than a baby, and they went away over to the west in a big red ambulance he bought with his university pay. He would live, somehow. He didn't live anywhere, with the kid. They slept in the red ambulance, picked up other travellers, camped on beaches under squares of flapping canvas, were dirty and bitten and, finally, happy.

Once Wally walked barefoot along a hot, terrible beach north of Perth, trailing after Jim who was looking for a creek. Wally had forgotten his hat and his father hadn't noticed. That night the little boy was in fits, spewing; his body was racked, his eyes rolled back in his head and Jim was seized with mortal fear, less of death than of the dumb face of Ruth. He threw the child into the ambulance and sped to the nearest town, his heart beating and stinging in the backs of his hands, glancing sideways at the flat creature beside him on the front seat. The doctor took one look at the ragged man, wild-haired and burnt black, and said to the nurse,

'Give the kid gamma globulin. It could be hep.'

It wasn't. Wally had a history now: 'Once I walked a hundred miles in bare feet,' he would relate long after

96

to his mother, who had many times imagined him ill, wrapped sweating in rags on some stranger's kitchen floor while his father ranted at the table behind him; 'and I got heat inzaustion and they gave me three needles in my bum.' Wally was thin and dirty with little muscles like string and pearly down in elegant whorls along his backbone.

Meanwhile, Ruth knew that if she were not to take out her guilt on Laurel she must find company, people to pick loose the threads that bound the burden to her. She dragged the kid in her glasses to the big house she had heard talk of. She walked in the back gate and saw a woman, a solid brown-skinned big-muscled girl in a flowery dress, bending over the vegetable garden yanking up weeds. They had seen each other at one of the meetings, perhaps. The dark woman looked at Ruth.

'Help,' said Ruth. 'Can I come and live here? Have you got a…'

The dark woman stood there with her feet balancing squarely on two great blocks of bluestone, an uprooted weed dangling from her left hand.

'Come inside and we'll have a cup of tea,' said Scotty.

Logically, Jim got busted for dope. There was no one with the money to bail him out, and they would have taken Wally away from him had not Ruth got on the train and come for the kid. He was a wild little boy.

He had never eaten off a plate in his life: he knew that the most reliable joy to be had was a packet of hot chips against the chest. He was burnt to a crust, and his foot-soles were thickly callused. His blue eyes penetrated. He had reverence for nothing, as his father had taught him. His response to discipline was to show his bum. But when his mother came to get him, a strange thing happened. They took one look at each other and fell in love. He would sit on her lap while she smoked, and slip his grubby little hand under her shirt and flip her breasts this way and that, his face a dream of content-ment. He would stroke her face with his hard paw, sing to her in his croaky voice: 'Woothy, my Woo,' he sang, swooning on her bosom.

Laurel was too big to be cuddled and too proud to ask for it. She stood about wretchedly in doorways. Scotty tried. Scotty loved her, there was no doubt, in the tentative way in which we love other people's children, fearful of rejection, even of mockery, loving without rights, thanklessly. Scotty's love was awkward, and intellectual. Laurel would bring to Scotty the teacher her difficult questions.

'Scotty, is Robinson Crusoe a myth or a legend?'

'Scotty, got any idea how to draw a hamster?'

'Scotty, do you believe in changelings?'

'In what?' said Scotty, who was reading the paper.

'Changelings. When a baby is born and they swap you for another baby and nobody knows.'

'I don't think they make mistakes like that in modern hospitals.'

Laurel made a quick movement of impatience. 'Not in *hospitals*,' she said. 'Fairies come and take you away. And put an ugly fairy baby or goblin instead.'

'Better not let your mother hear you talking about fairies,' said Scotty casually. She looked up at the girl's round face on the other side of the table.

'I was reading this book,' pursued Laurel, 'and it said, Once there was a mother and goblins had stolen her child out of the cradle. In its place they laid a changeling with a thick head and staring eyes who did nothing but eat and drink.'

Scotty laughed, then saw her false step. Laurel's face was stricken. 'Are you worried about it or something?'

'It sounds like *me*.'

'Oh Lol.'

'It *does*. A thick head and staring eyes.'

'I love the way you look.'

'You're only saying that to make me feel better.' Laurel's gaze was relentless.

'I once heard another story,' said Scotty carefully, dredging it up from memory, 'about a man who had two children. I think he was an Arab. One child was handsome and charming and popular, and the other was plain and clever. And another man came to visit, and while he was there he saw the two children and noticed how different they looked, and he asked the father, "Which of your two children do you find more beautiful?" thinking he would have to say "The elder". But the father thought a while, and finally he said, "He whom the heart loves is ever the most beautiful".'

Laurel said nothing, looking steadily into Scotty's eyes, but Scotty could see the flexing of iris as thoughts passed through her solemn head.

'I also eat too much,' said Laurel at last.

'You are *not fat*.'

'My *face* is fat.'

'It's puppy fat.'

'Yours wasn't.'

'I still eat too much,' said Scotty, whose empty plate was encrusted with muesli.

'Why do some people eat a lot and stay thin, like Wally, and other people eat the same amount and get fat, like you and me?'

'I eat more when I'm miserable,' said Scotty. 'Anyway we are *not* fat.'

'Wally said I was fat. He said it at school.'

'Wally is a shit.'

'No he isn't.' Laurel went red. 'He just doesn't want me to be his sister when there are other kids around.'

'Well, isn't that shitty?'

'He probably can't help it,' said Laurel. 'He's not proud of me.'

100

'*I* am.'

'But you're not in my *family*.'

'I can't change that,' said Scotty, and looked away.

'No matter how much you love me,' Laurel bored on doggedly, 'you can never be my real mother.'

'I know,' said Scotty.

*

Breakfast fiddled with, lunches in brown paper bags, the two children straggled off across the park, Laurel casting looks over her shoulder to where Ruth and Scotty stood at the gate watching, still in their pyjamas. The Italian boys from over the back came jostling round the corner and absorbed Wally into their group, leaving Laurel to drift on alone. The red ribbon on her top knot shone at them until she turned the corner past the milk bar and disappeared. The women sat down on the stone step.

'Remember when we had only Lol?' said Scotty. 'And I taught her to read, and we did the comic books, and she used to come and sleep with me?'

Ruth gave a brief laugh. 'No good thinking about that now.'

'But isn't it weird how Wally's changed everything. Lol used to be a happy kid. Now she moons round after you all the time. It's so important for Wal to be tough—he won't have a bar of her. I think it's sad.'

Ruth scrambled over to her open bedroom window and reached in for the packet of Drum on the table. The effort of forging thought into speech made her short of breath. Whenever she spoke of the troubles of her life, her accent broadened and she clipped her words off short. Her face came forward bearing the mirthless grin of resignation, neck awaiting the yoke. 'Wal's lived most of his life on a beach,' she said. 'He's not used to girls, or havin' a sister.'

There was a silence. The school siren went for nine o'clock, and the sunny street was empty. What a fine pair they looked to the boiler-suited gardener turning on the hoses in the little park across the road: one short, one tall, sitting carelessly on their front step dressed in cotton, forearms resting on knees, feet bare upon the smooth brown-and-yellow-tiled path. The man waved good morning to them and they saluted back.

'Another hot one?' he sang out, bending down with his spanner to the hidden taps.

'Looks like it,' they chorused.

The man moved across the park, setting free one after another dense mists of spray shot through with faint rainbows, mauve, yellow and green. Through the floating cloud slashed the postman on his bike and held out a fan of letters to them at the gate. Scotty jumped up to take them.

'Whacko! Pension day,' said Ruth. She hung the

cigarette from her bottom lip and ripped open the narrow envelope, scanning the cheque for deductions.

'Money for nothing,' joked Scotty, drowsy in the sun and late for work. 'I should have had a kid after all. Given up teaching.'

'You call that nothin'?' snapped Ruth. 'Bein'a mother in this society?'

Scotty did not like being corrected. 'Hmmmm,' she said in her wry voice. 'Just the same. It would have been different for me, if I'd had a kid now. It's a different kind of decision these days from what it was before the women's movement, when you had yours. If you had kids before the penny dropped, you're in the clear, aren't you. Proved yourself both ways.'

'What do you mean?' said Ruth suspiciously. She drew hard on her cigarette, baring her teeth and hissing in the smoke.

'Just a thought.' They paused, in a slight tension. 'Anyway,' Scotty went on, 'what about the idea we talked about last night, before we started fighting? Why don't we collectivise the house money?'

Ruth extended one long leg off the side of the path and poked about in the dirt with her toes. 'I dunno.'

'I think we ought to. I feel ashamed that I never realised before how much more I get than you.'

Ruth fired up at once. 'Ashamed? I don't *want* you to feel ashamed!'

'Well I do! I feel ashamed! Aren't I allowed? Is feeling ashamed counter-revolutionary or something?'

Ruth clamped her hand to her jaw and removed the cigarette. All the life went out of her voice as she said, staring out across the sunny road, 'I'm sick 'n' tired of havin' my hand out to the rest of you.'

'Tsk. Don't look at it like that.'

'It's a bit hard not to.'

'Why don't you get a job?'

'Nah,' said Ruth. 'I have to *be* here when the kids get home. The hours are no good. They can't come home to an empty house.'

'We could organise it,' said Scotty. 'That's all it needs—organisation.'

'Nah. When it comes to the crunch, the only people you can trust with your kids are other people with kids.' Ruth flicked away her butt, stood up and stretched, thrusting her chin forward as if presenting her face to the elements, and showing the thick sandy hair under her arms. In that position she looked like a ship's figurehead.

'Life's a struggle,' she recited, letting out a sharp sigh and dropping her arms.

'All shall be well / And all manner of things shall be well,' quoted Scotty, to sustain the philosophic moment and to conceal the faint sting of hurt from Ruth's last remark. But Ruth darted an irritated look over her shoulder as she opened the wire door and said,

104

'I hate that sort of religious shit.'

The ceasefire was over.

* * *

Alex believed the whole of western civilisation to have been justified by the invention of the saxophone. He played rhythm guitar in a rock and roll band. He was small and neatly made, with long, hard fingernails, pink Jewish lips, and bags under his eyes which, when he was very tired, tinted themselves a delicate shade of lilac. He drank too much coffee, too black, and read and practised all night because he couldn't sleep: his blood was nervous and alert. Sometimes, past midnight, Ruth would hear him beating away softly with one foot in time with his playing. He liked there to be a guitar in the room, even if it was only leaning against a wall. In the kitchen, if he wasn't playing, he was shelling peas into a saucepan, sharpening the knives, or gouging away with a rag at the tin of dubbin to polish his old brown shoes. He was never bored. Wally, who broke things and ran outside, made Alex quiet and wary, but Laurel he took into the room where the piano was and taught her to pick out a bass line with one finger.

'Frequency means...often-ness,' he would explain to her.

'Often-ness,' repeated the little girl thoughtfully.

105

'Why don't you teach her *Botany Bay*?' said Ruth, sticking her head round the door.

'I don't know it.'

'You've been culturally imperialised.'

'I know,' he said. 'I bet I have more fun than you do.'

*

After Ruth had stamped out of the house meeting and banged her bedroom door behind her, Scotty and Alex had been left at the table staring at their hands. The stillness of the dry yard crept in through the back door. A cricket scraped in the mint round the gully trap.

'She can't stand you, Scotty, can she,' said Alex.

Scotty, who had turned very red and stiff during the argument, forced out a high, difficult laugh. 'We used to be like *that*,' she said, holding up one hand with two fingers tightly crossed. 'She'd put food in my mouth so I didn't have to get sticky fingers.'

'What happened?' Alex tilted back his chair, reached behind him for the acoustic guitar, and began to pick at it.

'She started hating me.'

'But these things are never one-sided. There must have been a reason.'

'You tell me and we'll both know,' said Scotty with a stubborn, ill-tempered grimace. 'She doesn't like my tone of voice, she says.' Scotty disliked analysis; she wanted things to be just so, and for everyone to agree with her without wasting time.

'Is it something to do with this house? You found it. You got the upstairs room.'

'*She* could have had the upstairs room if she'd wanted it.'

'You run a pretty trim ship, Scotty. Signs on the wall and so on.'

'Anyone can put a sign on the wall.'

'Yes, but they don't, do they?'

'There's nothing to *stop* them.'

'Don't do your block.' His hand shivered to make vibrato.

Scotty twisted her mouth, half closed her eyes and drummed her fingers on the table in a pantomime of irritation. 'You know something?' she said. 'When the other house got sold, Ruth cried for a week. I said to her, "Ruth, you *must stop crying*. We have to *do* something." And she'd say, "Oh, don't talk about it. I can't even bear to think about it." She was *hopeless*. She was talking about squatting and being a stay-put widow, and that sort of bullshit. Everyone but her and me had full-time jobs, so I had to go out looking by myself. And I couldn't find anything big enough for the whole seven of us, so we had to split up. And you know what she said to me in one of these fights we're always having now? She said, "I'll never forgive you for the way you were at the end of Rowe Street. You were so cold and efficient—you didn't seem to care. And for me it was the end of the world." I was stunned.'

'What *was* good about that house?' said Alex. He kept on picking away, his face open and attentive.

'Oh...for Ruth it was special, you know. She dragged herself out of that mess with Jim, and he took off with Wally. She fixed up her room, and planted her vegetables, and started up a new women's group. It was a big household. Rosters. Telling life stories. Signs! *When was the last time you saw a man round here with a broom in his hand? Revolution begins in the kitchen.* The kids were everybody's kids—Laurel and Sarah's daughter used to call each other "my sister". We thought everything we'd theorised about was coming true. Breaking down old structures, as we used to go round saying in those days.'

'It almost sounds old-fashioned,' said Alex.

She laughed awkwardly and turned her face away from him. 'It was a home, I guess,' she said. 'We were always laughing and singing and drawing pictures of ourselves. We loved each other. We couldn't wait to get home at night.'

In the quiet, the steel strings quivered and the guitar belly resounded warmly.

'I'm jealous,' said Alex.

'Don't worry. You pay later,' said Scotty bitterly. 'Look at us now.'

*

Madigan accepted the cigarette because he thought that was what people probably did. He puffed amateurishly at it, roving round the room and expelling the smoke in a flat slice over his chin. He felt blunderous, as if he were occupying too much of the available space. The conversation was not successful: his voice seemed to him too loud, or too tentative, or too emphatic. In desperation he darted his myopic eyes round the kitchen in search of a new tack.

'What's in that bottle?' he bellowed. 'Gin?'

'It's Scotty's,' said Alex. 'She calls it a mood improver. Pretty dangerous one for someone who's in a bad mood as often as she is.'

Madigan gave a hoot of nervous laughter.

'Sit down,' said Alex. 'Make yourself at home.'

'I will in a minute,' said Madigan. He sat on the very edge of a chair, lumped his legs under the table, and rested his large forearms in Sphinx position across the cloth. His cigarette was at last sufficiently consumed for an attempt to be made at graceful disposal. He stabbed it into the ashtray and withdrew in relief, brushing one hand against the other. He had butted it imperfectly, however, and it continued to smoulder, releasing a thin grey column of smoke to the ceiling, betraying his discomfiture as surely as cooking smoke betrays the outlaw to his pursuer. Alex reached out one hand and crushed the butt against the china.

Madigan edged over to the record player and squatted down beside the pile of records. 'Hey! Billie Holiday! Whose is this?'

'Scotty's,' said Alex.

'They all belong to all of us,' said Ruth at the same moment. She was crouching down to sort out rotten oranges from good in a wooden crate under the kitchen bench.

'No—I mean who bought it,' said Madigan.

'Nobody in particular,' insisted Ruth. 'They're everyone's.'

Madigan, with his back turned, rolled his eyes and clenched his teeth. He squatted there on his large haunches for ten minutes, working slowly through the stack, examining the covers, making a light hum of attention to the task.

'I hear you're making a record,' he said at last.

'Yeah, that's right,' said Alex.

'Who's producing it?'

'Bloke called Everett Walker.'

Madigan let out a snorting laugh. He stood up and drifted back to the table where Alex had picked up a biro and was doing the *Age* crossword. 'Do you *like* Everett Walker?'

Alex looked up. 'Do you mean personally, or his work?'

'Any way you like,' said Madigan hastily, confused.

'He's all right, I suppose. We haven't got much choice, at this stage of the game.'

Madigan pointed his lips and put the fingers of one hand on the tabletop, keeping the other safely in his jacket pocket.

'I don't—there's something—he talks too much,' he said. 'He's got one of those mellow voices that seem to grow on you, like moss.'

Alex laughed.

Madigan drew a deep breath. 'Don't you think he's a bit—sort of—'

'What?' said Alex, interested.

'I can't stand him!' burst out Madigan. 'He gets hold of bands like yours, that have a rough, human sound, and he makes them sound like a hospital trolley!'

'Wow! You're a master of simile!' said Alex, in genuine admiration.

Madigan looked at him sharply. 'Do not patronise me, my handsome young fellow,' he said with a peculiar frowning smile, 'or I shall lash you with my clever, cutting tongue.'

Alex started to laugh, and gestured with his hands palms upwards.

'But how can you *work* with a bloke like Everett Walker?' cried Madigan in another spasm of agitation. 'I mean—how do you prevent him from riding rough-shod over you?'

'Oh, you just give him the steely smile and the cold shoulder,' said Alex airily. He picked up his guitar and held it across his lap.

'You old softie,' said Ruth, who had been taking in this male pantomime. 'You never gave anyone the cold shoulder in your life.' She laughed.

'I did so,' said Alex.

'Who?'

'Oh, I dunno. Someone.'

'Everett Walker actually came to our house once,' said Madigan.

'Into your actual *house*?' said Ruth.

'And sat at our actual table, in our actual kitchen, and drank an actual cup of tea.'

'Gosh,' said Ruth.

'I thought you couldn't stand him,' said Alex.

'Oh, he didn't come to see *me*,' said Madigan. 'He was talking to Tony about some deal or other. Anyway I tipped the sugar bowl over his head.'

'You *what*?' Alex stared.

'Oh, he started bandying about words like zen and off the wall and laid back and talking about Jah, and everyone was listening to him so idolatrously that as usual I was at the end of my tether. So I grabbed the sugar bowl and tipped it over his head and ran out of the house.' His eyes quivered behind the lenses, like fish in a tank.

Ruth and Alex laughed with new respect. They had gathered closer to Madigan where he sat and were gazing at him with such shameless curiosity that he edged further away and fidgeted the salt and pepper about on the table. Alex ran off a few absent-minded riffs. 'Well,' he said, with a turned-down smile. 'That answers the question I was going to ask you, I guess.'

'Which one was that?'

'That's why I asked you over, as a matter of fact. I thought maybe you'd like a bit of—you know—session work.

'Who, me?' said Madigan. 'You mean, on your record?'

'Yeah.'

Madigan uttered an incomprehensible sound somewhere between a laugh and a shriek. 'That'll teach me to keep my smart cracks to myself,' he mumbled. He flung up his arms and clasped his hands behind his head, squeezing his eyes shut and opening his big mouth very wide. As they stared, his face became quite peaceful. The grimace relaxed, a smile curved the lips, the eyes opened as if he had had a refreshing sleep.

'Want to have a blow?' he said, colouring up. Ruth went back to the sink and put the plug in.

'OK. Have you got your harps?'

Madigan leaned down behind him and produced the pillow-case from its hiding place round the corner in the hallway. 'What'll we play?' he said. 'Down at my place they always want to play *Rose of San Antone*.'

'Don't know that one,' said Alex.

'Play *Love Hurts*,' said Ruth.

'That's American imperialism, isn't it?' said Alex.

'Yeah. But it does, doesn't it. Hurt,' said Ruth.

Alex laughed. 'I wouldn't know. Would you?' He looked at Madigan who was burrowing among the metal.

'Love's just romance, isn't it?' said Madigan uncertainly. 'Hollywood, and that?' He chose a harmonica from the jumble and ran it back and forth between his thrust-out lips. 'We don't have to play a song,' he said, sipping at the instrument. 'Let's just mess around. You could do hand-claps, Ruth.'

'Go on! Do *Love Hurts*!' cried Ruth. She flung the dishcloth into the sink. 'You know how it goes, Alex! Like on the record!'

Alex nodded, planted his feet against the table edge and chopped out a deliberate rhythm for her, which Madigan, inspired by this unexpected burst of exuberance, punctuated with elegant flourishes of breath.

I know it isn't true
I know it isn't true
Love is just a lie
Meant to make you blue

sang Ruth. She was smiling with half-closed eyes; she twirled around on the red concrete floor, clapping her hands and swinging her long limbs with a lively vigour

114

and cheerfulness. Was this the same Ruth? thought Alex; the one who wore the harness of gloom? She was moving like a queen, light-footed, open-handed, full of pleasure and grace.

'*Love hurts / Love hurts / Love hurts...*' Ruth's voice faded out, just like the record, and the three of them laughed and looked away from each other in that mixture of embarrassment and almost tearful joy that comes after wariness has been shed.

'That was nice!' said Madigan. 'It's like those country pubs you go to up the backblocks of New South Wales—they always have a blond woman with big tits and a microphone, and she sings like this'—he threw back his head and bawled—'*LA International Airport! / Where the big jet engines roar!*'

Before Ruth could react to this remark, the door opened and into the room stepped Scotty in her crépe-soled shoes, home from work and not in the mood. She stumped silently across the room heading for the loaf of bread.

Madigan looked up, blinking. 'Hullo!' he said brightly. 'You must be Scotty. I've heard about you!'

'Have you indeed,' said Scotty, hacking away at the bread.

Madigan stared at her in puzzlement. No one spoke, but Alex saw, with a quickening of the heart, the blade of light that flashed from Ruth's eyes into Scotty's heedless back.

'We were just having a blow,' said Madigan. 'Want to join in? Sing a bit?'

'You don't give up, do you,' said Scotty, keeping her eyes on what she was doing. She slammed the fridge door shut with her knee and tramped out of the room with a bulging sandwich in her fist.

'Yikes!' said Madigan. 'Did I say something wrong?'

'The boss comes home,' said Ruth.

'I thought you didn't have bosses in these sorts of houses,' said Madigan.

There was no answer. Madigan could not read their expressions, and chattered on regardless. 'Still, I suppose it must be hard to cater for everyone's tastes, in a commune. One person's under the shower singing *Old Father Thames* and all the others like new wave.' He laughed, looking from face to face.

'It'd take too long to explain,' said Alex.

'Here come the kids,' said Ruth.

*

'Know what there is on the way to school?' said Wally, getting reluctantly into the bath.

'No. What,' said Scotty.

'A big drawing on a wall. Of a great big dick.'

'Oh.'

'With balls 'n' everythink.'

116

'And sperm coming out?'

'No. Just a little hole at the end. But guess what. I come past there with Laurel, and guess what. I said, Look at that great big dick. And *she* said, That's not a dick, that's a *thumb*. Even with that *knob* on it 'n' everythink!' He laughed, screwing up his face and hugging himself with glee.

'Oh well,' said Scotty. 'Here. Wash your face.' She wrung out the washer and held it out to him.

'Has it been on your cunt?' said Wally with his slow, insolent smile, not taking his hands out of the water.

'No,' she said.

'Do you know my dad?' said Wally.

'No. I've never met him.'

'He's *great*.'

'Is he?' She shook the washer, waiting for him to take it.

'He wouldn't like you,' said Wally.

'How do you know?'

'Oh, he just wouldn't.'

Scotty looked at him meditatively. She took one step forward and stood over him, the washer steaming in her hand. He seized it hastily, but his rapid wipe did not erase a knowingness which made Scotty glance behind her to the empty doorway.

'Get a move on, will you?' she said. 'I have to go and pick up Laurel from tap. You can stay here. But

117

listen to me. You are *not* to go down to the creek, do you hear me?'

'Aw. Why not?'

'Because you're clean, that's why. And because the creek's polluted.'

'Big fat bum,' whispered Wally into the washer.

'What did you say?'

'Nothin'.' He stood up, gripped the side of the bath with both hands, and clambered out on to the mat. He shook himself like a dog, his little penis flipping up and down.

'Where's Ruth?' he said.

'At the laundromat. She'll be home any minute.'

'*Good*,' said Wally daringly. He took the towel from her hand and buried his grinning face in it.

To the watery strains of *The Good Ship Lollypop* and the tremendous reverberating thunder of forty little girls in metal shoes, Scotty climbed the stairs of the warehouse and lined up with the mothers in a damp corridor. The music stopped, the big door opened at the end of the hall, and out streamed a river of children, their heads at breast-height to the waiting women; they flowed steadily along through the narrow-run, shoving like sheep in a race. Scotty searched for Laurel, but all the faces pointed with determination in the same direction, not looking up, the elbows working like pistons. There was Laurel's big red ribbon.

'Lol!' Scotty put out a hand and tapped the child's shoulder. 'How was it?'

Laurel's face was trying hard not to collapse. 'Awful,' she said. She inserted herself between Scotty and the wall and sheltered there from the surging bodies. Scotty took her hand and looked down at her pink-framed glasses, her large feet in the shoes with their jauntily-tied ribbons.

'What do you mean, awful?'

'I couldn't do it.'

'But it was only your first time.'

'They went too fast for me. They put me in the back row and told me to copy the girls in front, and I couldn't see the teacher, and the kids next to me knew how to do it and they *laughed* at me.' She buried her face in Scotty's belly.

The crowd was dispersing rapidly. 'Bloody shits,' said Scotty. She was ready to kill. With her arms round Laurel she threw up her head and stared round for the teacher. Out came a little old woman in tap shoes, clacketing along the floorboards. She saw Laurel and Scotty and a look of concern changed her face under the thick creamy make-up.

'My dear!' she cried, clicketing and clacketing up to them. 'Oh, you're crying! I *thought* you weren't having much fun. Is this your mother, darling?'

'Yes—I mean no,' sobbed Laurel, taking her face off Scotty's trousers and trying to wipe her eyes.

'But don't worry about crying!' said the teacher, tremulously dabbing at Laurel's cheeks with her hanky. 'It's good that you cried! It shows how much you care about doing it well!' Her legs were hard with muscle, but quivering with age and fatigue. Her eyebrows were plucked to the thinnest line and lipstick had leaked into the wrinkles round her mouth. Beside her Scotty was a giant in her flat runners. Laurel's freckled cheeks were flushed, her glasses awry, but she had stopped crying; her curiosity at seeing the teacher at such close quarters distracted her from her humiliation.

Scotty said to the teacher, 'We'll be all right. We'll probably be back next week.'

Laurel squeezed her fingers imploringly.

'If we feel up to it,' added Scotty.

The teacher nodded and watched them anxiously as they went, padding and clacketing, along the empty hall.

Laurel heaved a sigh. 'I thought it was going to be fun,' she said.

'Aren't you supposed to take off the shoes?' said Scotty, as Laurel clattered down the stairs and out on to the footpath, holding her hand.

'I don't even care,' said Laurel. 'I hope nobody thinks I'm ever coming back here. Because I'm not.' She tore off the shoes and flung them into the back of the car.

'Adversity is very character-forming, I'm told,' said Scotty. They got into the front seat.

'What's adversity?' said Laurel.

'Hard times. Hard life.' Scotty turned on the ignition.

'Can we go and get a souvlaki?' said Laurel.

'You'll get fat, like me, if you don't look out.'

'Oh, why do you even *worry* about it?'

*

On a balmy, greyish afternoon when autumn breezes buffeted, Madigan dozed the hours away under the eiderdown. Each time he woke he was surprised to find he had been asleep: the angle of the light had shifted along his flecked wall, the household noises had ebbed into silence; into his mouth ran the sweet taste of fresh saliva. After school when the stampeding feet woke him for good, he stumbled down to the park with two of Myra's boys and played kick-to-kick with them till teatime. Their cries were mysterious to Madigan, who winced and shied away from their rough bodies because of his spectacles. 'Jezza!' they shrieked, plunging after the tight leather; 'Thommo!' with a dying fall.

'You boys better get home,' said Madigan at last. 'Myra will be wondering where you are.'

He was always surprised when they obeyed him; he did not realise that they liked him because he addressed them in exactly the same tone of seriousness that he used in talking to grown-ups, instead of acting out for other adults present the little play called 'Talking to

Children'. They pelted off ahead of him, and he saw them ripple over the zebra crossing and vanish round the corner.

When they had gone the air was utterly still. Swallows passed like a handful of flung pebbles. Darkness swarmed under the thick-leafed trees. It was as if darkness and not light were the force. The orange gravel of the intersecting paths was lurid with the struggle of darkness against light. The water of the lake was not water but some thick, gluey substance incapable of movement. Ducks forced their way across its surface, moving in formation, dragging a wake of arrowheads. Madigan began to walk quickly home, keeping close to the fence.

He reached the hollow lighted kitchen with relief. Myra was standing at the stove with an apron tied round her waist. She was talking with animated gestures to one of the unfairly glamorous girls from over the road whom Madigan privately referred to as 'the girls with the bee-stung lips'.

'It had this great big skirt?' said Myra, stirring, 'made with—' (she groped for the word) '—*abundant* material?'

Madigan always felt like bursting into applause when he witnessed one of Myra's raids on the inarticulate. He sat down at the table and unbuttoned his jacket.

'Madigan,' said the smallest boy. 'When we start eating, will you keep sitting next to me?'

'Why, Harry?'

'Because I like you, and I like you to sit next to me,' said Harry.

'All right.'

'Thank you,' said the boy in a soft contented murmur, and leaned against Madigan's side.

'Don't mention it.' Madigan blinked and blinked, half-dazzled by the bare bulb which dangled over his head. The great chimney-place opposite him was stuffed with old newspapers. The girl with the bee-stung lips drifted out of the room in a patchouli cloud, layers of worn crêpe swaying round her booted ankles. A faint odour of dope clung around Myra's solid person as she delivered the steaming pan to the centre of the table.

'Oh, not soup *again*!' groaned the eldest boy, putting his spoon down with a crash and turning away in disgust to rest his face in the palm of his hand.

'You should be grateful to your mother,' said Madigan severely. His glasses fogged up in the steam that rose from his plate. He began to transport the soup to his mouth, tilting the bowl at the correct angle and closing his lips round the spoon so as not to make slurping noises. Myra served the three children and herself. 'Mmmmm! Flavoursome soup, Myra!' said Madigan in the cheerful, encouraging tone of a husband in a television commercial. Blinking rapidly, he pursed his lips for the next spoonful. The bored boy, watching Madigan's exemplary table manners, suddenly laughed out loud. His mother dealt him a ringing blow to the side of the head.

'Get to your room!' she shouted, flushing with embarrassment and rage. 'How dare you?' She glanced at Madigan who was staring, bewildered, spoon raised, dimly aware that this unpleasantness had been provoked by some oblivious act of his own. Harry had dozed off against Madigan's arm, and the middle boy, having seen the lie of the land, was shovelling soup into his mouth as silently as he could, darting his eyes left and right as his brother left the room red-faced and furious, holding back tears.

The children were dispatched and the two grownups finished the meal in silence.

'Where *is* everyone?' said Madigan.

'I'm here,' said Myra, looking into her empty bowl.

'No, I meant the others. Tony and the blokes.'

'I don't know. Gone to play, I guess.' Myra went over to the sink and turned on the tap.

'Don't wash up,' said Madigan vaguely. 'I'll do it later.'

'It's all right. Don't you get sick of washing up, doing it all day?'

'They sacked me, didn't I tell you?'

'What for?' Myra already wrist-deep in water, reddened again with indignation on his behalf.

'Oh, I'm a pretty slow worker,' he said. 'They don't have to give a reason. Probably got someone with ambition.' He laughed and rolled his eyes at her.

'Well, I think that's terrible.'

'Who's staying home with the kids tonight?' said Madigan.

'Me.'

There was not even a hint of resentment in her voice. Her patience drove Madigan to distraction. Why didn't she jack up? Blokes never did anything unless forced. He'd better buy her a book, or something.

'Are you going out?' she said.

'Oh, I might. Later on.'

She ground away with a piece of Jex at the saucepan bottom. Madigan looked at her feet in the loose sheep-skin boots, patiently parallel at the sink, and felt like tearing his hair.

'What about a game of Scrabble?' he said with an effort. Myra turned round with a shy smile. She must have been pretty once, but her face had puffed up and her belly had gone and she was always announcing diets and then lying about it: the bee-stung girls would walk in and find her giggling guiltily behind the kitchen door with a slab of carrot cake in each hand and crumbs all round her mouth. Her eager kindness excruciated Madigan. Someone like him couldn't afford to be around sadness like hers.

'I'll play,' she said, 'but I'm not very good at it.'

Madigan turned away to hide the gnashing of his teeth, and pulled the maroon cardboard box out of the drawer. Myra wrung out the dish-mop, banged it firmly to separate its white strands, and hung it on the tap under the sign Tony had put up saying *Washing glasses in soapy water makes the beer go flat*. She sat down opposite Madigan, blushing with pleasure, and Madigan laid out the board and the little wooden racks with his thick graceless hands which always trembled slightly, and they played a slow game, painstakingly placing the creamy tiles in their squares, cogitating without haste, for neither of them possessed the killer instinct. The alarm clock sat upon the table with a woollen tea-cosy to muffle its tick; its face looked foolishly askew up the spout-hole.

From the front bedroom came sounds of struggle, fierce giggling, feet running away. The big front door slammed violently and Harry set up a wail. Madigan glanced up but Myra, soothed by mental effort and adult companionship, went on placidly contemplating her move, one eye squinted against the smoke of the joint which Madigan had declined to share. Harry's weeping, moving very slowly closer, was becoming heart-rending.

'Is it good for him to cry like that?' said Madigan, shifting in his seat.

'Of course,' said Myra briskly. She did not take her eyes off the board.

'But—to go on forcing it out, long after there's nothing left? So his whole body aches?'

'He'll stop when he's sick of it.'

Harry sidled in, swollen-faced. 'I got no one to play with, and no one to look after me,' he said thickly.

'You're not the only one with that problem, me lad,' said Myra, chin in hand, still not looking up.

'Steady on, My!' said Madigan, shocked and impressed by her tough tone.

Harry slid up to his mother's legs. She took him on to her lap, one hand outstretched with a tile ready to place. She slipped her other hand up under his jumper and tickled his sweaty back. He took a big quivering breath, let it out again and relaxed against her. Madigan winked at him and clicked his tongue, but Harry was not ready to smile.

'Would you pay CON?' said Myra.

'Oh…I don't think so. I don't know,' said Madigan, who was slipping, himself, into a faint dream of comfort.

'Tsk. Come on. Don't be wishy-washy. Would you *pay* it?' She swung her head up to look at him, her eyes blank with concentration.

'Harry,' said Madigan. 'Run out to my room and get the dictionary, will you?'

'He can't read,' said Myra.

'It's a big thick book with red and yellow stripes.'

127

Harry trotted away and returned with the right book.

'Good on you,' they cried.

He smiled tremulously and slipped back on to Myra's knee. Absently she soothed him, playing all the while.

'Those big boys are bullies,' she said, 'sometimes. It's one of the things I should try to knock out of them.'

'Maybe the events of their lives will knock it out of them,' said Madigan.

'*I'm* an event in their lives.'

Madigan sat hypnotised by her certainty, her deft handling of what to him were looming imponderables: children's distress, their nastier character traits, the future. He recognised the danger signals in himself: a slight swooning sensation, a physical comfort drawn directly from the fact that she achieved this balancing without even looking up from the game. He pulled himself together and stood up abruptly from the table.

'I think I'll go out,' he announced.

Myra looked up, aware that by some false move she had forfeited his company. 'Thanks for the game,' she said, completely without irony.

'*Don't thank me*, Myra,' he ground out, and bolted from the room.

*

Dennis shot things at weekends. He told Ruth she lived with dilettantes who were up themselves. His smile looked more like a snarl. Ruth took pride in being the only one who could handle him when he was drunk. Once Scotty had walked into Ruth's room without knocking and seen them lying together: Dennis's face was turned towards her over Ruth's shoulder, his white teeth were bared, his eyes glazed. For a second Scotty thought there was murder: then she realised they were fucking. His pale blue eyes looked at her but did not see. She ran.

Dennis never stayed for breakfast, but slipped away to work as soon as it was light. Anyone who had left a bedroom door ajar might at the instant of waking glimpse the loose dangle of his arm, sense the quiet disturbance of his passing, a blondness, thread of tobacco smoke, sponge of boot-sole.

Dennis was always leaving. Ruth, who longed to be his ally in a struggle larger than their own lives, who longed to be like him (blunt-minded, phlegmatic, wary of easy levity—virtues, she imagined, of his class), did not protest; but sometimes when he knelt over her to say goodbye, when he searched her face, she felt herself swell and grow puffy with sadness. She reproduced, not consciously but by the osmosis of desire, his ungrammatical speech, his flat vowels and truncated cadences. She called people 'mate', professed impatience with subtleties: 'I can't stand all this stuff about colours,' she would declare, folding her arms over her flowered apron. 'All this shit about "Is that puce?" "No, it's more like magenta", when it's really just purple or dark red.' She roughened up her manners and her childhood memories, so that one Sunday when her father came to call, Alex and Scotty were agape at his rounded, jovial tones, his casual bandying of literary references.

Ruth waited for Dennis at night, long after Laurel and Wally had dropped off and the ironing was done and the kitchen set to rights. Towards midnight her ears were tuned to the scrape of the back door on the matting. She would put on her flannelette nightie and her glasses and get under the blanket and open *Labour and Monopoly Capital* and begin the plodding task, the mountainous journey she conceived between her history and his. He would come in and find her asleep with the light on, the book still upright on her chest between her loosened fingers.

She captured him one Sunday.

'Stay,' she said. 'Oh, go on. I'll get you breakfast in bed.'

Half laughing, half frowning, he gave in. She kicked off her felt slippers, galloped to the shop for milk and bread, trotted to the kitchen and set up the little wooden tray for him. Scotty stumped in and cut up a grapefruit with a serrated knife, facing straight ahead to discourage conversation. Ruth was in the state of silly over-cheerfulness seen in those whom love has made happy. She swung her hip to bump against Scotty's as they stood side by side at the bench and hissed,

'Been fuckin' all night. Stink like an alley-cat on heat.'

'Charming.' Scotty, who had slept the righteous sleep of the loveless, turned a slow look of distaste upon her. 'What was that crash on the front verandah at one o'clock this morning?'

'Oh that!' said Ruth with a grin. 'Dennis was a bit pissed 'n' we had a fight 'n' he ran out 'n' jumped on me pushbike. Bent it.' She giggled. 'He give me some money to get it fixed, but.'

Scotty's mouth curled in disgust. 'What an oaf,' she said. 'I hate men.'

'Get yourself a real one,' said Ruth cheerfully. 'Not one o' them soft-talkin' Carlton types.' She hoisted the tray breast-high and strode out of the room.

'Yoo hoo!' she yelled. 'Tea-oh!' She pushed the bedroom door open with one knee, and stopped. Dennis had slipped back into slumber. A narrow strip of sunlight lay across his broad face, across the pillow and the cream-coloured blanket with its faded blue stripe. His hair was messy and yellow. A grey shadow fell around his eyes, described a curve across the breadth of his cheeks. He was breathing very quietly.

Bunches of dried flowers (dead flowers to Scotty, who had no use for souvenirs) hanging from the curtain rod along the kitchen windows were symbols, for Ruth, of what had been and what she alone was faithful to. Where had the laughter gone? In the old house they had laughed till they ached, in convulsions of hilarity: joints before breakfast, spiky electrocuted haircuts, improvisations in foreign accents, gentle family jokes (Laurel trying to remember Moby Dick and coming up with 'Dick Shark'), acid trips when the little girls had clowned to entertain them and Ruth and Scotty had lain against the furniture weeping with laughter, dying with laughter.

The institution of Telling Life Stories had gone swimmingly at the old house, once a week, in each of the bedrooms in turn: the cups of tea, the packets of Iced Vo-Vos and Chocolate Royals, the knitting, the open fire, the horror stories that any childhood will turn up: 'My father read my mail and found the contraceptive pills.' 'He was driving so fast I thought I could just open the door and jump out.' 'When I got home from school my mother...my mother...' 'He came into the bathroom and I was in the bath with my sister and he said, Who did it?' 'They took her away and I never saw her again.' 'She died.' 'I was afraid to open my mouth.'

For Scotty, this was over. They had been through it once, once was enough; the sound of her own voice droning the ossified facts disgusted her. But Ruth wanted it again, to show Alex how it was done; she wanted to keep something alive, to build a bulwark against the draining away of the recent past through neglected channels. Scotty gave in ungraciously, Alex out of curiosity. Ruth went first. She told and told, with that dull gleam of eye, mirthless smile, slow mastication of detail: and Scotty fell asleep, a crime for which Ruth would never forgive her. 'I was drunk,' said Scotty afterwards, grinning with shame. 'I got bored! I slept for two hours and when I woke up you were still in grade three.' Alex gave an embarrassed laugh, and flipped a tortoise shell guitar pick between his fingers. Ruth glared at the floor. Scotty, trying to make amends in the name of domestic peace, offered to tell her own story the following week. She produced an elegantly edited version of her thirty years, studded with ironic jokes against herself and tailored stories of travel in countries the others had never been to: 'The music went on for three days and three nights; I had pneumonia and a nun looked after me; we crossed the river at dawn; I went into this room and there was more coke on the table than you'd ever dream of seeing in all your life; when I got to his place and saw the mattress on the floor I thought, Let me *out* of here!'

At the end of it the others sat in silence, frustrated and confused. They were none the wiser about Scotty's personality—or rather, she had not given away any little weaknesses, which was of course the unspoken reason for these sessions: let us bare our weak points so I won't have to be afraid of you any more.

Scotty was seriously bored. It had much less to do with Ruth than Ruth imagined. She suffered from boredom as a condition. She would sink into it, would be up to her neck in it, without having a name for it. She had no way of concealing it, of making herself gracious in spite of it. At school her kids held it at bay: their sexual restlessness she understood, and they made her laugh with their strangled English; but at home it came creeping into the marrow of her bones. She ate too much, furtively devoured Easter eggs, muffins, half packets of Vita-Weats thick with butter in the middle of the night on her way back from the lavatory. After these binges she would fade into anxious sadness, an obsession with the deed; guilt, shame, lack of energy; a desire to turn back time, to sleep away what she had done, to be free again of the load taken on; fear of ugliness; weariness; despair; self-disgust at the failure of will. It was part of the condition that she could not talk about it. She would wander round her room, try on all her clothes, grieve because none of them hung loosely on her; she would unbutton her overalls, drop them to her ankles and dully examine her body in profile, holding her shirt up under her breasts. She longed miserably to hack off the offending flesh, to have it surgically removed in some secret clinic. If Ruth came striding into her room while she was lying there after work, black-faced, struggling with this loathing of herself, hiding behind a book, if Ruth sat down and sighed comfortably and pulled out the packet of Drum, Scotty's discourteous grunt of greeting was the best she could do. She wanted to scream, *Shock me*! but she couldn't be bothered. Ruth would take the crude hint, gather up her tobacco and papers and matches and go quietly, closing the door behind her. It was all on Scotty's terms. Nothing Ruth said succeeded. Scotty was sick of the old fooleries. She wanted nastier mirth, to say the unforgivable, to purge herself of her disgust. With her ignorant certainties she rudely crushed Ruth's stirrings of intellectual curiosity.

'The Great Wall of China can be seen from the moon,' said Ruth.

'Oh bullshit,' said Scotty crabbily. 'It can't, can it, Alex?'

'Why don't we buy an encyclopaedia?' said Alex the science graduate, the diplomat, refusing once again the unenviable role of Solomon.

When Scotty went on the night train to Mildura for her term holidays, she bought a postcard at the station of a certain local geological formation called The Walls of China and sent it to Ruth with the inscription, 'Reckon you can see this from the moon as well?' Ruth was hurt and cross; but some dregs of rough affection in the message touched her obscurely, and she looked at the postcard front and back for a long time and then stuck it in *Labour and Monopoly Capital* as a bookmark. None of them ever looked up the disputed factoid. Indeed, the peculiar angle of the dismal little piece of information made it hard to classify: Wall? Moon? China?

Ruth enjoyed starting sentences with 'us deserted wives', 'us single mums', invoking with a sniff and a twisted grin the sisterhood of adversity. Into her bones had sunk wisdoms such as *All good things must come to an end*, *Life's a struggle*. With casual relish she related tales of disaster and pain. 'If there was one thing Sarah didn't need, it was a caesarian, after the childhood she had.' 'They took one look at him and he was full of it—they just sewed him back up again.' Over the morning paper she narrowed her green eyes, pursed her lips, drew in hissing breaths, gave ironic nods of suspicion vindicated, and made vague political predictions. 'The pressure's buildin' up,' she would say, ominously. 'The lid's gonna blow off any minute.'

'We had the radio on while we were fuckin',' she told Alex in the kitchen. 'An', the news come on and they announced the PKIU only got a five dollar rise. Dennis's cock went all limp. We couldn't go on.'

She gave an odd, triumphant laugh of excitement, her eyes gleaming dully.

'Wouldn't it have been better to fuck more, instead of less?' mumbled Alex, who was flossing his teeth. 'That way you would have been defying the badness, if you see what I mean. Making a stand for human contact.'

'What are you, a hippy?' said Ruth.

136

At that moment Alex noticed Dennis, eyes down, coming up the path between the kitchen door and the lavatory.

'Look at that blond head,' Alex remarked enviously to Ruth. 'I always think blonds are more...sort of *blessed* than other people.'

Ruth stared. 'What sort of an idea's that? How can a Jew come out with a thing like that?'

'There is a faint flicker of Nazism in it, isn't there,' said Alex, sawing away with the waxy cotton.

'More than a flicker!'

'I nearly said *holy*, actually,' said Alex, laughing. He was not fazed by ideological rebukes, though goodness knows he had enough of them to contend with in this household, of every conceivable brand.

Alex and Scotty came out the front door on their way to the gig. Ruth's bedroom light was still on.

'Bloody house meetings—just an excuse to get stuck into each other.'

'No wonder she hates you,' said Alex, stowing his guitar in the back and buckling his seat belt. He revved the motor and they swooped away on to the road. 'Look at you—all dressed up to go out on the town, and she's in her room bawling.'

'Oh, don't *you* start!' said Scotty. 'Why does everyone think I've got no feelings?'

'You do seem to cope,' said Alex.

'*Somebody* has to cope! And once you start, they expect you to cope for them as well, and you're never allowed to drop your bundle ever again—and then the buggers hate you and tell you you're authoritarian!'

'Maybe that's why we hate our fathers,' said Alex in his maddeningly reasonable tone.

'Oh shut up.' Scotty stuck her elbow out the window and slouched in her seat. The car, open to smooth streams of night air, cruised down Punt Road and crossed the river.

Outside the back door of the pub, Scotty said, 'I might just hang round out here till it starts.'

'Don't be silly. Come inside and talk to us.' Alex was standing sideways on the step with his guitar case in his hand.

'No. I don't want to look like a moll.'

Alex laughed and went in without her. She leaned against the wall and looked up and down the street. A tram passed, light and square as a cage, making the asphalt tremble under her feet. She thought about Ruth at the meeting, her grim face and set jaw, her determined pessimism, the way she dragged on the cigarette as she ground into words the grist of her resentment. Strung tight as new fence wire, Scotty's shoulders ached with self-control. She let out a mean sob.

'Shut up, idiot,' she snarled out loud.

Under the rows of knobbily pruned plane trees came three Aborigines, a man and two women, stumbling cheerfully home. The man saw Scotty leaning there in the dark with her hands in her pockets, knee bent, one foot back against the wall, and sang out,

'Hul–lo my son! How you going?'

'Good thanks,' she called back, knowing that her voice would betray her sex and embarrass him.

'Ooooh! It's a girl!' shrieked one of the women, and they all went off into gales of laughter. 'Sorry!'

'It's all right,' said Scotty, blushing.

'Good night love!' They rolled on by, a jolly trio smelling pleasantly of beer.

'Good night,' said Scotty.

She turned on her heel and went round the corner and into the pub.

It was crowded and red-dark inside. She shouldered her way to the bar and ordered a scotch, propped herself with her back to the bar, and downed it in one gulp. Ruth swam away. Scotty hated parties, but liked pubs, for here she had no social responsibilities: everything was paid for and the deal was clear. She did not like social drinking, or beer, or wine. She liked to get rapidly and efficiently drunk on something hard and dance it all off and go home alone, and anything more was just somebody else's fantasy. 'Drinking is between me and the bottle,' she had said once when Ruth and Dennis offered her a beer at the kitchen table. 'No one else has anything to do with it.' The memory of this remark made Scotty flinch with shame. She hated talking about herself, and imagined such statements being repeated mockingly behind her back.

She found herself a spot between the bar and the cigarette machine and drank quietly through the first awkward, cold bracket, when the speckled concrete floor was bare and she was not going to be first. She watched the roadie's blond head gleam green in the light over the desk, the swing of his arm as he brought the cigarette to his lips, his hands hovering over the board sneaking the volume up with each song; she saw the band one after another twist in their earplugs as the sound turned bitter and clattered tinnily among the rafters; she drank Scotch until the taste of it no longer withered her and it started to do its job on her stiff righteous joints; she drank scotch and ice, and by the break she was oiled up and loose. She waited.

She felt the ripple of attention run through the crowd, a turning of heads and bodies towards the lit stage, and away they went again on a riff she knew by heart from hearing it a thousand times through her bedroom floor at night. She battled down to the front of the band where she could watch Alex, whose face took on a resoluteness, a sweet grimace of concentration: her feet were lifted surely off the sticky floor and she was dancing, whisked up and washed away in the oceanic commotion of sweating bodies, in the same unfailing bliss engendered by hot swimming pools full of screaming kids. She heard Alex pick up the riff and his teeth flashed as he began to grin to himself and she was grinning too and before she closed her eyes she saw sweat flying round the drummer's head like a little net cap sewn with pearls and she closed her eyes, she was herself for herself with no skin to hold her in, and to the wincing man in distorted spectacles standing pressed against the side of a speaker box her face was as open and tender as that of someone *blissed out* on some *mind-expanding drug*—that naked face and powerful body—better steer clear of her, she looked dangerous.

Watching her, Madigan suddenly thought of a film he had once seen, *Gentlemen Prefer Blondes*, in which two women, one dark, one fair, both big and graceful as racehorses, strode like colossi among puny millionaires or muscled giants whose personalities had been pumped into their biceps. An odd run of expressions passed across Madigan's face: sourness, envy, admiration, suspicion. She wasn't stupid, that girl dancing with her eyes shut: she had just slipped her moorings, and he wished he could do the same.

The music stopped and she opened her eyes, giddy, not knowing which way she was facing. She had her back to the stage and tears all over her face, and there was someone standing in front of her talking to her, a Hawaiian shirt and glasses and shoulders hunched inwards.

'Do I know you?' she asked stupidly.

'I came to your house once,' he said. 'To visit Alex.' He was peering down at her through ugly spectacles. His eyes were watery and seemed to want to burst through the glass: his lashes spread against the lenses. She thought perhaps she remembered him, his childish shoes, feet pointing straight ahead.

'Why are you looking at me like that?'

'I'm not,' he said. 'It's the curse of all bespectacled people. People think you're looking at them funny, or sexy, and you're really just trying to see who they are.'

'I'm having a bit of trouble with that question myself at the moment.'

'Which question?' He stared right into her eyes, perfectly serious.

'Oh, never mind. You wouldn't understand.'

'You're not crying, are you?' He glanced nervously left and right to see if anyone else had noticed that she was still giving the odd sniff.

'Want to make something of it?'

He laughed a peculiar gusty laugh, hyuk hyuk, too loud, as if someone had formally told a joke. His breath smelled sweet. 'Oh, I wouldn't take *you* on,' he said.

'Why not?' she said in a pugnacious tone.

He composed his features into a debonair expression. 'I keep running into strong women who are looking for a weak man to dominate them, as Andy Warhol said. Although I hate Andy Warhol and all that New York stuff.'

Scotty laughed. 'I'm looking for someone to flatten, actually.'

'You can flatten me.' He spread out his arms. 'It'd be easy.'

'Don't be a dag.'

'Well, buy me a drink, then. Please.'

She looked at him sharply. He had a very thick, white neck. 'On the bite, are you.'

He nodded and blinked.

'The direct approach always works on me.' She wiped her cheeks with the back of her hand and he followed her to the bar.

'Do you actually like this sort of music?' His oyster eyes, distorted by the spectacles, narrowed as he raised the glass of beer.

'Of course,' said Scotty indifferently. She sucked a mouthful of scotch through the ice.

'It's not to my taste,' he said. 'At least...I don't think it is. Still...everyone's much more professional in the city. Specially this side of the river.' He stuck out his chin, expecting contradiction, but she merely replied,

'Why don't you get proper glasses?'

'I had some once. Gold.'

'What happened to them?'

'I had this girlfriend up north, and at the vital moment I failed to make a declaration of passion, so she jumped on my glasses and went to Europe.'

Scotty laughed. She looked him up and down. He stuck one hand in his pocket and with the other tilted the glass so that a few drops of the beer ran down his throat. He pretended to whistle, looking behind him.

Alex came shouldering through the mob, sweaty and shiny.

'G'day, Madigan. What's the matter, Scotty? I saw you crying. You looked really small.' He grabbed the back of her hair and yanked at it.

'I'm OK,' said Scotty. She nodded at Madigan. 'He's not sure if he likes the music all that much.'

Alex turned to him. 'Oh yeah?'

Madigan took a deep breath and rushed it. 'It's too New Yorkish, and violent. And decadent. What's it got to do with Australian people's lives? Why don't you play music for ordinary Australians?' He was panting, staring earnestly into Alex's face.

'If you want to see some "ordinary Australians",' said Alex, controlling himself with difficulty, 'come out to a Saturday night gig in Ringwood sometime, mate.'

Madigan fixed him insistently with his protruding eyes. 'No, not them. I mean the mums and dads. Mr and Mrs Normal.'

Scotty butted in, clenching fists and teeth. 'Mr and Mrs *Normal*? This is rock and roll, you *dag*.'

She cast Madigan a look that would have floored him had he not summoned up all his nervy, scrupulous tenacity to deflect it: he was older than Scotty, and more romantic, and probably even more bitter. Their stares locked, then dropped apart in a kind of hostile respect. Scotty turned abruptly and strode away towards the lavatory. The men raised their eyebrows at each other.

'I like Scotty,' said Madigan who, to Alex's stupefaction, now showed no sign of agitation. Completely composed, breathing in a regular rhythm, Madigan held up thumb and forefinger a hair's breadth apart. 'That cool she's got—it's about *this deep*.' His attention wandered. Alex saw his gaze blur, slide, then suddenly sharpen and focus. 'Any chance of a blow with you blokes?' he said in a fresh tone, hearty and humble.

Scotty sat fully dressed on the lid of the end toilet, scowling into her fist. On the back of the cubicle door some ignoramus had printed *I hate the overalls brigade lesos and all dumb womans libb chicks*. Scotty drew a black texta from her front pocket and replied *Perhaps if you wore overalls yourself it might reduce the pressure on your spleen signed Miss Piggy Veterinarians' Hospital*. She stood up, rested one knee on the toilet and raised her face to the rigid louvre windows which gave on to the playground of the crèche next door to the pub. Through the chicken wire she stared at an abandoned swing: it moved faintly on dull silver chains, clinked faintly in the apricot night air.

The outside door of the lavatories, flung back by a drunken hand, crashed against the basin, letting in a bright blast of music. A harmonica squealed. Scotty sprang up, ran out the door and plunged back into the red crowd.

It was Madigan working away at the centre microphone, a stooped, shock-headed, self-possessed figure, both hands to his mouth, the lead wagging: his eyes were squeezed shut behind the flashing lenses, his fingers flicked open and cupped shut. He was peeling off high, sheer ribbons of sound. Everyone was dancing.

When the crowd straggled out, it took with it the fragile romance of 2 a.m. Without the music, everything showed its decrepitude. The carpet was hopelessly stained and damp, worn thin as skin between the tables. The musicians, their glamour turned off with the lights, stood about randomly looking ordinary-sized and ill-tempered, cheated again of emotional recompense for their outlay. Scotty leaned against a wall and watched two girls in vinyl pants and lurid make-up loitering with intent between the stage and the door of the band room. The girls were in the way of the roadies who staggered round them, knees bent under the shared load, muttering curses. Scotty stepped up to Alex.

'You be long?'

'Don't think so. I'll just pick up my pay.'

'What's the matter with Whatsisname?' She jerked her head at Madigan who was crouched at the side of the stage.

'Not feeling the best.'

'Is he OK?' Scotty stared at him. Alex shrugged and made a motion of playing a violin. Scotty approached the hunched figure. He saw her feet and jumped. 'Are you all right?'

'Sort of-ish.' He looked up.

'Are you ill?'

'Probably got flu. Or something.' He straightened up with a confused attempt at a laugh.

'Let's go,' said Alex, coming up behind. 'Want a lift home, Madigan?'

'Well...' He looked around him. 'Do you think anything else is going to happen here?'

'Oh for Christ's *sake*,' said Scotty. 'I have to go to work tomorrow. Yes or no. Don't drag the chain.'

Madigan followed sheepishly, dawdling past the closed door of the band room with its strip of light along the floor.

When they stepped out on to the esplanade, the clock on the pillar said two thirty. A line of palm trees held up their stiff fingers against dark blue air which smelt of fish and salt.

Madigan had begun to shiver dramatically. Scotty shot him a cross look.

'Let's drop in at the Greek's for a coffee before we take you home,' said Alex. 'Are you too sick for that?'

Madigan shrugged, knowing he did not have a choice. He twirled the pillowcase this way and that; the harmonicas clacked.

Alex was greeted familiarly by the owner of the cafe as he served them at the high glass counter.

'Do you always come here after gigs?' said Scotty.

'Always. It's open day and night.'

'The whole twenty-four?'

'Yep. It's a *rock and roll* café.'

Scotty thought of the morning to come, children in the kitchen and the classroom, and longed again for the exhausted camaraderie of night workers.

'Now you know why I'm always half stunned in the mornings,' said Alex, tipping a sparkling river of sugar into his cup. He glanced at Madigan, this spectre he had invited to the feast, and tried to kick things along.

'This is a rare moment,' he said, 'seeing Scotty awake in public at this hour of night.'

Madigan did not reply. He looked quite pathetic, hitching his thin jacket and the collar of his lairy shirt up round his chin.

'Comes on sudden, doesn't it,' said Alex. He stirred his cup with a vigorous motion.

'Come and stay at our place,' said Scotty on an impulse, half to make Alex laugh, half meaning it. 'We'll look after you till you're better. What are you doing out on the streets at night in this condition? Don't you get looked after at your place?'

'Are you kidding?' said Madigan.

'Bloody hippies,' grunted Scotty with a righteous expression.

'They're all right. They're not running a hospital, you know.'

'It's the test of a collective household,' said Scotty primly, 'whether you get looked after when you're sick.'

'Ah yeah. They told me over in Prahran to look out for people like you,' said Madigan. 'Communes, and that.'

'What would they know about it,' said Alex with a blithe laugh. 'They're hopeless, south of the river. Sit round the kitchen table blowing joints all day, nothing gets done.'

'Come to us, then,' said Scotty, beginning to clown. 'We'll make you a little bed, won't we Alex? All nice, with clean sheets smelling of mothballs. Freshly squeezed orange juice. Fizzy vitamin pill.'

'Yeah, that's the stuff,' said Alex.

'And we'll put the orange juice through the—what is it, Alex?—the *sieve*, like Ruth does, so it won't be, you known, too *strenuous* to drink.'

Alex tipped his chair back and laughed out loud, but Madigan, unable to gauge the exact edge of her tone, watched suspiciously. 'I think I'm probably too weak for the treatment,' he said. 'Maybe you'd better just drop me off home. I'll get something at the chemist tomorrow.'

'Get stuck into the ginseng, pal,' said Scotty, swilling the dregs round in her cup and not looking at him. 'Isn't that the big cure over your side at the moment? Or is it comfrey?'

'What's wrong with comfrey?' Madigan rallied. 'Myra at our place makes fritters out of it. I *like* comfrey.'

'Myra makes 'em, does she?' said Scotty. 'And what do *you* make?'

'Me? *I* can't cook,' he said, caught on the hop.

'Know what the first thing is?' continued Scotty smoothly.

'Learning how to boil water. Or—no. First you have to find the kettle.'

Nobody laughed.

After they had dropped Madigan home, they turned into Punt Road and flew back across the river.

'Bit rough on him, weren't you?' said Alex.

'Rough! He was just trying to provoke me!'

'No he wasn't! Listen, I've been to his place. You ought to go down there. Un—believable.'

'What happens?'

'They couldn't even get a market roster going. The men objected to being asked to come to a meeting about it. The blokes sit up at the table like Lord Muck while the women run round waiting on them.'

'You're starting to sound like a lackey of the feminists,' said Scotty. 'Are there any kids?'

'A couple, I think. It's the sort of house where you hear terrible sickening bangs and screeches from the other room. And their mother never goes out at night.'

'What a horror show!' said Scotty, gasping with enjoyment. 'You mean that actually still happens?'

'Look, Scotty—it's time you got out of Fitzroy! Nothing's changed, in the outside world!'

*

Ruth drove, and Scotty and Sarah crouched at the back doors of the Holden poised to spring out at the chosen spot. The first couple of times they were jerky with fear and excitement, so hard did their blood thump. Ruth sat behind the wheel, leaning forward eagerly to watch the dim figures bobbing up and down against the wall like buoys struggling in water. By the fifth time, out in Hawthorn, far from home, their actions had become fluid and swift. Up came Scotty's arm, sprayed the huge words in her elegant left-handed script, while Sarah squatted, hopping crab-wise along behind her under-lining in one smooth continuous flow. They sped away from each finished sign in a euphoria of silent laughter. It was like falling in love again in the dark. All their antagonisms dissolved, their eyes shone.

'Don't you want to have a go, Ru?'

'Oh—I'd be too slow. I haven't got such nice writing as Scotty,' said Ruth shyly, dying to.

'You do the next one with Sarah,' said Scotty. 'I'll keep watch.'

151

'Here's a nice white bank,' said Sarah. Ruth swung the car into the side street and turned off the motor. 'Come on, Ru.'

Ruth grabbed Scotty's can and slipped out after Sarah. She was so eager that she started without checking that the nozzle was facing away from her, and squirted herself on the face and neck.

'Eeek!' she screeched, brushing pointlessly at herself.

'Leave it, leave it!' said Sarah. 'Go on! Your turn!'

Scotty heard them and glanced over. At that moment the divvy van flashed past along Glenferrie Road. None of them saw it. Sarah and Ruth, weak with laughter, were stabbing away with the cans at the punctuation which Scotty insisted be perfect. Scotty neglected her watch again to check the spelling, and round the corner swept the divvy van.

'Get in! Get in!' yelled Scotty, twisting the key in the ignition. Sarah tumbled into the back seat and Ruth ran to the driver's side, pushed Scotty over and took hold of the wheel. Of course it was too late. The van blocked their exit from the narrow street, its lights blinded them, its doors burst open and two policemen strode down upon them, huge in the blaze of white and flashing blue.

'Oh God, look at 'im,' whispered Ruth. The first one was blue-faced, big-jawed, a nightmare cop, eyes invisible under the peak of his cap. He shoved his hand through the window and seized the keys out of the ignition.

152

'Whose is this car?'

'My husband's,' said Ruth.

He saw immediately that there were no men in the car, and his tone changed. The younger one stood silent on the other side of the car.

'Where *is* your husband? Does he let you out on the streets after midnight, does he?'

'My husband's in jail,' said Ruth, staring straight ahead through the windscreen with narrowed eyes. 'And I wouldn't ask his perm—'

'I see. And where are your children while you're out at night engaged in this sort of activity?'

'At home. Well looked after. *Mate*.' Ruth turned her black-streaked face up to him with a stare of concentrated hatred.

He met her gaze. 'I'm Inspector Nunan, of Glenhuntly CIB,' he said. 'We'd like you to follow us to the station.'

He passed the keys back to her and she snatched them rudely.

The divvy van sped away and they followed.

'Our rights. Our rights. What the fuck are our rights?' hissed Scotty. 'I knew we should have read the Civil Rights booklet before we left.' She began to giggle.

'Shut up, Scotty,' said Ruth. 'This is serious.'

'What a disaster,' said Sarah, whose freckled face in the helmet of curls looked white and small. 'We didn't even finish the sign.'

'Forget that now,' said Ruth. 'That's the cop shop there, isn't it? He's goin' in. Well, what *are* our bloody rights? Do we have to say anything? You two are the fuckin' intellectuals round here.'

'We can't very well *deny* anything,' said Scotty. 'They did catch us red-handed.' She and Sarah were on the verge of a fit of laughter.

'Can't you two shut up?' said Ruth, furious.

'I thought *you'd* know all that stuff about rights, Ruth,' said Sarah. 'I thought communists knew all that stuff.'

'I'm just a fuckin' deserted wife, mate,' said Ruth grimly, pulling up next to the divvy van outside the town hall. That's all I know about.'

'Well don't start bloody playing the violin about it, for Christ's sake,' said Scotty.

'What are we going to *say*?' said Sarah.

'I'll do the talking,' said Scotty.

The young policeman had inspected the boot of the car and was standing beside it with the keys in his hand when they came out the door to go home. They nodded to him and got into the car. Ruth backed it out of the drive and made a big U-turn.

'Look at that dingbat,' said Sarah. Scotty glanced back and saw the young cop standing with one arm raised, waving goodbye to them like an idiot country boy waving to a train. The two of them began to giggle weakly, disgusted with themselves. Ruth took no notice. She planted her foot and away they went.

*

Ruth stumbled out of her bedroom and heard shouts of laughter from the kitchen. Scotty was transforming the night's debacle into a comic turn for Alex's entertainment.

'And round the corner, to put it bluntly,' she was saying with her wry smile, 'came Inspector Nunan of Glenhuntly.'

'To put it bluntly,' said Ruth from the doorway, 'we made fuckin' idiots of ourselves. In the cop shop we were pathetic.'

'Oh, come on, Ruth! It's not all that serious!' said Scotty. 'Can't we even get a laugh out of it?'

'It's all right for *you*. You've got enough money to pay the fine.' Ruth slopped coffee into a cup. 'Where are the kids?'

'Out in the street,' said Alex. He stood up from the table, picked up his bowl and ran it under the tap.

Ruth took a tearing drag on her cigarette and breathed out a long plume of smoke. 'Did they get anything to eat?' she said to nobody in particular.

'No,' said Alex. 'I'll go and call them.'

'Oh, don't bother,' said Ruth with a sigh. 'I'll do it in a minute.'

155

'*I'll* do it,' said Alex.

He could be heard yelling at the front door. Ruth and Scotty drank their coffee with downcast eyes.

'I'm goin' down the Prom for the weekend with Dennis,' said Ruth. 'An' I'm leaving the kids here.'

'All right,' said Scotty ungraciously.

With a great stampeding the two children ran in at the door and flung themselves at the table. Alex went about the business of serving them, singing to himself to cover the dismal sound of burnt toast being scraped. Laurel seized the plate of toast, divided the pile into two equal parts and shoved one in front of her brother. The red bow on top of her head wobbled vigorously as she ate. The children crammed the slices into their mouths and chewed loudly with much smacking of lips and champing.

'Why don't you two shut your mouths when you chew?' said Scotty in a surly tone. 'It nearly makes me sick to listen to you.'

They glanced up at her, puzzled, and went on gulping and gnawing.

'Lay off 'em, Scotty,' said Ruth. 'Just lay off 'em.'

'I *live* here,' said Scotty. 'It's awful, the way they eat. Why don't we teach 'em?'

'Don't be so fuckin' bourgeois! You never used to think table manners were important!'

'Things change,' said Scotty. 'They're not babies any more.'

156

'*You've* changed!' said Ruth. Out came the Drum, the tense rolling. 'You know what's happened to you? You've turned into a boss. You're an individualist.'

The children stopped eating. Wally kicked Ruth under the table, and pointed at Scotty.

'She's fat,' he announced.

'Shut up, Wal,' said Ruth. Her mouth flickered, and Scotty had to turn away to hide a tremor which passed across her lips. 'I'm goin' away for the weekend, you kids. Scotty 'n' Alex are goin' to mind youse.'

'Ohhhh! Ru–uth! Why can't we come?' cried Laurel.

'Cause you can't, matey, 'n' that's that. Come up to my room 'n' talk to me while I get my stuff ready.'

The family trooped out the door into the hallway, keeping their eyes down.

Alex, who had observed this scene from the other side of the bench, came and sat down beside Scotty at the devastated table. Their eyes slid sideways and met. Scotty gave in.

'Fat, am I,' she said.

'Miss Piggy,' said Alex.

The pair of them lolled there, faces to forearms on the tabletop, and laughed till tears came to their eyes.

'Oh God this house is gruesome,' groaned Alex. 'It's driving me nuts.'

'Don't say nuts. I might want to eat some.'

'Driving me bananas, then. Oh, sorry.'

157

Fresh spasms bowed them down.

When they looked up, Wally was standing on the kitchen step, half hiding in the doorway.

'I'm gunna make a rabbit hutch,' he said.

'But you haven't got a rabbit,' said Alex.

'But one day I might save up and buy one, from selling bottles.'

Laurel pushed into the room behind him. 'Are you going to make it now? I know where the hammer is. Can I make it with you?'

'Sure,' said Wally magnanimously, heading for the shed. 'You can hold the nails.'

Laurel's face dropped. She looked back at Scotty and Alex sitting at the table. They were speechless, but Scotty raised one clenched fist and shook it encouragingly. Laurel ran out the back door with an expression of single-minded determination.

'Starts young, doesn't it,' said Alex.

From the shed came the splintering of wood and voices raised in eager discussion.

'See youse,' shouted Ruth from the front door, and crashed it shut.

'I think she's going down to the beach to make up her mind,' said Alex.

'What about?'

'Whether to leave or not.'

'*Leave*? Oh Christ. I thought we'd made up our minds to stay here and knuckle down to it.'

'It?'

'It, it, IT. The flaming collective necessity.'

'Oh, I'm sick of talking about it,' said Alex. 'I'm going into my room to have a little practice.'

*

People were setting up a fair on the scrubby football oval at the northern end of the gardens. Scotty pedalled across the lumpy grass and propped in front of a display board at which a girl with her back turned was struggling to pin some flapping posters to the caneite. Scotty, still holding on to one side of her handlebars, leaned across to help the girl restrain the poster. The girl glanced at her.

'Miss,' she said in a very soft voice. 'Remember me, Miss?'

Scotty stared. The girl was young, only about nineteen. Scotty remembered something…faces and desks flicked past like pictures in a book, a fine dust of chalk entered her nostrils and fizzed there, chalk dust packed the whorls of her fingertips. A faint effort throbbed. The girl was dressed anonymously in jeans, a dark blue windcheater and cheap running shoes. She looked Greek. Not one of the beauties. A blunt face, lips permanently parted, a mouth breather. Eyebrows clumsily plucked and half grown back. Back row on the right, under the map. Not Effi. Effi's friend.

'Soula, Miss.'

A great, rare smile broke over Scotty's face. 'Soula.'

They were both laughing silently, looking right into each other's eyes. Then they stood still and studied each other.

'Miss. If anyone ever asks me about teachers, I say, Miss Scott was the best one I ever had.'

'Oh Soula.'

'Really Miss! I loved your class. I learned stuff.'

'We had a lot of laughs, anyway.'

'Miss! Seriously!' A shadow of earnestness passed over her face.

'It must be seven years ago,' said Scotty.

'Long time, Miss.'

'Yeah.'

'Miss. Do you remember when you took us to see *The Summer of '42*?'

'Yes. And remember when we went on the excursion to the tombstone maker and Vito dropped the big block of marble on his toe?'

Soula turned aside to laugh, covering her mouth with her hand.

'What's everyone doing down here in the park?' said Scotty.

'It's the Tribune fair, Miss.'

'You can call me Scotty, you know.'

'Sorry, Miss—I mean—'

They laughed.

160

'It's the Tribune fair, Miss. I work for the Party.'

'Oh yeah? How long?'

'Three years.'

'How did you get involved?'

'My parents.'

Scotty stood over her bike and nodded. Soula's plain, direct, un-ironic gaze took in Scotty's pink trousers, the black shirt, the frivolous New York badges, the sparkling combs that held the hair back over her ears, the ears themselves pierced in several places with rings and studs. Scotty, at this casual mention of the Party, felt the beginnings of the same envy she swallowed every Friday night when Alex went home to his parents for dinner, to be present at the ritualistic lighting of certain candles in ways mysterious to her, exclusive.

'Do you ever see any of the old grade?' said Soula.

'I ran into Vito, actually, at the market, just before Christmas,' said Scotty. 'He told me he had to leave when he was in second form. Because some kids beat him up, or something.'

'He dobbed someone, Miss,' said Soula severely.

'Oh.'

'Miss, do you remember Tony Petridis?'

'Of course.'

'Well he's a junkie now.'

'*What*?'

'He's a junkie.'

161

'You mean a bad junkie, a real one, or just the odd...'

'Real one. He's a pusher.'

'But I only saw him—'

She had seen him a year before, loafing on the footpath outside Johnny's Green Room at two o'clock in the morning. She was drunk, staggering home after some gig or other, on her own and fearless with whisky. She would have walked straight past without recognising him had he not stepped forward and called to her, 'Miss!' He was huge, strong as an ox, a muscle builder, bursting out of his white T-shirt, but in his face still shone a calm seriousness, the courtesy and intelligence of the strictly brought-up Greek boy. His three friends stood quietly behind him in the shadow, watching. Exactly as she and Soula had done, laughing and then soberly curious, Scotty and Tony Petridis examined one another quietly and without haste, up and down. Each of them echoed with oblique shafts of memory, with the pleasant ache of old sexual imaginings, always contained by decorum and long ago forgotten. She had watched him from the high staffroom window. His soccer player's body—the triangular torso, low hips, short powerful legs—wove and swayed, graceful as a slow dancer, down in the rainy yard. Oh Tony. He reached out his arms to her that night: he took hold of her tenderly in his huge arms under the sickly neon of the poolroom, he held her firmly against his great

162

chest and kissed her on the mouth. A perfume of hash and sweat hung about him.

'You should see his hair,' Soula was saying. 'It's right down to *here*. And you know how he was always big? Well now he's *fat*. Do you remember Effi? She's a junkie. She's got a baby, even. The doctor reckons it might have been born with an addiction. It's like a cat, real skinny, sort of deformed. She can't get off it, Effi. We try to help her. She doesn't *want* to stop. But we won't let her go.'

Stupid with shock, Scotty listened to this litany, spoken with the same dull, gleaming-eyed fervour with which Ruth told her bad news. Who was this *we*? There was no *we* with power to prevent the rot.

'Do you think the posters look good, Miss?'

She tried to look. The posters, firmly attached now to the vertical board, showed what might have been expected—forests of fists raised, a banner-crowded sky, a suckling mother brandishing a machine gun: the whole panoply of worn-out symbols from which Scotty, like the rest, had learned to hope.

'Do you like it, Miss? Is it all right?' Soula's damaged eyebrows made an inverted V of anxiety.

'Yes, it looks great.' The teacher's tone of mechanical encouragement rolled smoothly off her tongue. Soula's face relaxed and she stepped back from the board.

'Thanks, Miss.' She was smiling. She was content.

When Scotty got home she climbed the narrow stairs to her room and lay on the bed. The air was as grey and dirty as if she had been told of a death. Some birds were singing unnaturally loudly on the tiles outside the window. She tried to cry; but she had talked herself out of that, too.

*

The beer glass was empty. No need for Madigan to feel in his pockets: that was it.

I like them, at home. Of course. I like them naturally of course. No one's ever allowed to dislike anybody these days. I do like them. I do, I do! But not when they play. They don't know how to build up a feel. It goes sloppy on them. God sometimes I feel old. I'm too old for dope, that's certain. Thank goodness. I must make a list. A list. I hereby resolve till further notice to avoid having lots of options. OK. A list. I wonder if I can get that old bloke down Gertrude Street to sell me the guitar case without the guitar in it. The neck is bent as any fool can see. If I practise more. Two hours every morning. Before breakfast.

He printed PRACTISE 10–12 DAILY on the first page of the exercise book. He crossed out 10–12 and replaced it with 11–1. Under that he wrote BE REALISTIC. Then GET SLIPPERS, PILLOW. He scribbled out SLIPPERS and printed THONGS.

Might be a couple that match in one of the boxes. VACUUM ROOM. Vacuum room. Moon. Loon. Tune, BUY RHYMING DICTIONARY. They say they've never managed to find a rhyme for silver, or orange. Funny. Both colours. Oh well, substances too. Objects. Ob*jects*? Mister Otis regrets. That he won't be around. Unnggggggg. I didn't like to just not turn up or say nothing, but ouch! By the time I'd contacted her I was a nervous wreck. I lost interest. She lost interest. Interest was lost. Hell, I wrote her a funny letter with drawings, surely that's reasonable enough value, BUY STAMPS. I try against ingrained habit and prejudice not to talk in riddles, BUY ENVELOPES, DO NOT TALK IN RIDDLES. PULL BED OUT AND LOOK UNDERNEATH. *I moved my bed into the middle of the room / Floating like an island in a sea of gloom.* Is that corny? Is it hackneyed? A battered ornament? Did I make it up, or did I read it somewhere? Does this happen to Real Artists? PRACTISE THREE HOURS DAILY. What happened to the list. *List of songs to do.* STAND BY YOUR MAN. Hyuk. That'll ginger up the feminists, DIAMONDS ARE A GIRL'S BEST FRIEND. Steady on. That's going too far. Next thing'll be foot-binding. 'In my profession I have learned that women can bear more pain than men.' 'Are you a doctor, sir?' 'No. A shoe repairer.' Hyuk hyuk.

He underlined THONGS.

On the colour television, high up on a shelf, two blurs were singing.

Hey Paul, I wanna marry yew
Hey hey Paula, I wanna marry yew tew

A man at the next table called out to the barman. 'Mate! Hey mate! Turn it up.' He tried to catch Madigan's eye. Madigan nodded.

'Swallows Juniors,' said the man. He raised his glass to the screen. 'Look at those kids.'

The barman scrambled up and tuned the set.

Trew lurve means planneen a life for tew
Bein' tewgether the whole day threw

they harmonised, beaming. The boy had bands on his teeth.

Madigan cleared his throat. 'Don't you think they're a bit young to be singing that sort of stuff?'

'No fear!' protested the man. 'Have to start early, in show biz.' He was smiling, as if they were his own children.

'But what would they know about true love?'

The man stared at him. His smile faded. 'They're *very talented kids*,' he snapped, and turned reverently back to the screen.

Madigan was getting that bursting feeling. He seized his pen and in a flowing hand covered the rest of the page with song titles. Madigan was working.

*

A fine powder of rain flicked in through the open doorway of the tram; it seemed to spurt out from the bending street lights. He got off at the corner of the gardens and mooched along in the dampness, heading for the only house he knew north of the river. There it stood at the apex of the triangular park, with its protruding attic window beaming light. The big front door was shut and he bashed it with the knocker. A moment passed, then the door opened a crack. A small fair-haired boy stood there with his hand on the lock.

'Good evening!' said Madigan.

The boy stared at him.

'May I come in?'

'Ruth's not here,' said the boy, looking past him at the darkening street.

'Is anyone else home?'

'I have to go to the shop,' mumbled the boy.

'What for?'

'Scotty said I have to get a tin of peaches.'

'Haven't you got enough money?'

The boy dangled by one arm from the latch of the door. 'Sometimes,' he said in a conversational tone, 'when it's getting dark and cars come along, well it might be too dark for the driver to see a little kid crossing the road, and he might...'

'Would you like company?' said Madigan.

'What?'

'Will I come with you?'

'All right.'

'Haven't you got any shoes? It's raining.'

'Come on.' The boy pushed his hand into Madigan's and dragged him across the road.

While Madigan watched, the child bought the peaches and selected for himself a packet of chicken-flavoured chips, which he devoured noisily, not offering to share, on their way back to the house.

'Won't you spoil your tea?' said Madigan helplessly.

The boy up-ended the packet into his gaping mouth, crushed the paper and dropped it in the gutter, and wiped his face on his sleeve as he heaved the front door open with his shoulder. He sprinted away down the hallway, leaving Madigan to make his own way into the house.

Scotty looked up as Wally flew into the kitchen.

'A bloke's here,' he shouted, a vein swelling in his neck. 'A great big bloke with glasses. Wanna see my drawing, Scotty?' He shoved the tin of peaches and a sheet of computer print-out under her nose. 'Guess who it's of.'

'I don't know,' said Scotty, not really looking. 'Is it Tom the Cabin Boy?'

Wally clicked his tongue. 'Does Tom the Cabin Boy,' he said with heavy sarcasm, 'have a red cape with a big S on it?'

'Hullo Scotty!' said Madigan. He stood just inside the door, knotting his hands, with the self-consciously interested expression of a tourist entering a museum. He was dressed in neat trousers, a tie and a cheap black jacket buttoned up to the neck. His large face looked benevolent, slightly puzzled, as innocent as a farmer's. 'Nasty damp weather, isn't it!' His manners seemed anachronistic, as if culled from a courtesy manual. Laurel put her finger between the pages of her book and gazed at him from behind.

'Are you looking for someone?' said Scotty, who was shifting sausages round under the griller with a pair of springy tongs.

'Oh, just a bit of human contact,' he said. He looked wildly at Scotty standing there in Ruth's apron, a meaner, musclier Myra, and suddenly his eyes filled with tears of self-pity and homesickness. 'It's so cold down here!' he said in a strangled voice.

'No it's not!' Scotty laughed. 'It's hardly even the end of summer!'

'I can't stand it,' he said. He took off his glasses and wiped his eyes with a neatly folded hand-kerchief.

'*Is he crying*?' hissed Laurel in a piercing whisper.

Madigan took no notice, but polished his glasses busily and resettled them in their ungainly position against his eyelids. A dark flush had spread from his cheeks down his neck and inside his collar.

'Want a gin and tonic?' said Scotty. 'Get the morale up a bit?'

At the thread of kindness in her dry voice he sucked in his breath and rolled his fishy eyes in a parody of self-control. Through the pinkish blur of his steamed-up glasses he saw the intent faces of the children. He could hear the cracking of ice, unscrewing of lids, ripple of liquids, a fizz.

'Here. A little mood improver,' said Scotty, and shoved a cold glass into his hand. It was too late to ask for hot Milo, but for a second he despised her for not having offered it. He grabbed the glass and guzzled at it.

Laurel, overcome with interest and the desire to draw attention to herself, shoved past Wally and took centre stage in the kitchen. She gave two affected, feathery coughs and threw her chubby limbs into a pose: one arm bent, hand at the waist, the other arm curved up to shoulder height with its wrist sharply bent and fingers pointing downwards at the floor.

'Do I look like a teapot?' she cried shrilly.

Dinner was well finished and the children long since sent to play before Madigan had ruminated his way through his plateful. Scotty fidgeted over the empty china.

'Is there any reason why you eat so slowly?' she said.

He shrugged, carefully removed a morsel of gristle from between his back teeth and laid it on the edge of his plate. 'There's a name for it,' he said. 'Fletcherism.'

'*Fletcherism?*' She laughed. 'Is this serious?'

'Some bloke named Fletcher reckoned you should chew each mouthful a hundred times. Actually, he said for a quarter of an hour, but I found that rendered me unfit for human company.'

'You mean you tried it?'

'For a while.' He placed his knife and fork alongside each other on his plate and sat back.

Scotty studied him in the remaining daylight. 'You're not…sick, or anything, are you?' she said.

'Homesick.' He tried for a laugh, but could only produce a dismal cackle.

Scotty was not used to being dumbly asked for comfort. Criticism was more in her line. What would Ruth have done? Ruth knew all about misery and sympathy and hot-water bottles and snacks served up on wooden trays.

'We could make a fire,' she said at last.

'Does the chimney work?'

'Of course it works! What do you think we do in winter?'

'How would I know,' he said drearily.

'Oh come on,' said Scotty, her short patience beginning to fray. 'Bear it like the bullocks.'

An anxious voice rang out from the front of the house. 'Sco–tty!'

'Ye–es! I'm out here!'

Not loud enough.

'Sco–tty!'

She got up and went over to the kitchen door and saw Laurel and Wally coming towards her along the dim hall. They were oddly quiet, moving hesitantly and very close together. Then Laurel saw Scotty and gave an exaggerated sigh, hand on heart, knees miming failure. 'Oh, thank God!' she cried with a shaky laugh.

'Did you think I'd gone out?' said Scotty, putting her hand on Laurel's shoulder.

'We came downstairs, and the kitchen light was off, and I thought—'

'We haven't even turned the lights on yet!' said Scotty. 'We were just talking. I wouldn't go out and leave you!'

The children looked up at her silently; even Wally was solemn with relief.

'Come on. I'll get you two into bed,' said Scotty. Over her shoulder she said to Madigan, 'How about you chop some kindling while I get this organised?'

She disappeared into the hallway.

Madigan kicked himself for not having confessed immediately that he had never chopped wood in his life. She would come back from the bedroom all bright and ready to start burning things and he'd be standing there like a shag on a rock, no wood cut, and she'd pause for a second as women do and turn on a slightly different smile and pick up the axe and do it all herself with him trailing along behind like a tin

172

tied to her ankle. Everything always moved too fast for him. What a rotten town. It wasn't even autumn yet. He'd have to buy an electric blanket. Maybe they had secondhand ones down the Brotherhood. Surely a secondhand one couldn't *be safe*. How many days might a bloke lie out there in his hovel before someone missed him and came looking for him and discovered his charred remains?

When Scotty came back she took one look at him and marched straight through the kitchen and out to the shed. He heard a dozen solid, rhythmical blows and back she came with an armful of split kindling, which she dumped neatly on the hearth at the end of the long room. Raindrops had made shiny streaks in her black hair.

'I'll do it,' she said, tossing him a neutral look. 'Last person here from up north spent hours breaking the kindling up into icy-pole sticks. Queensland people don't know how to make fires.'

Off the hook. 'Don't they?' he said. 'I'll have to think about that.' He was struggling with a wave of that smooth, insidious comfort that rinsed away his confidence. 'Blokes these days,' he said in a murmur. 'Competent young women like you…it can be rather a humbling experience.'

'Don't get *too* abject.' She skilfully constructed a fire and put a match to it. It took, and she squatted in front of it watching the flames run along dry sticks.

'I haven't lost the knack,' she said, and gave a little closed-mouth laugh.

'I like you, Scotty,' he said, surprising himself, for he had at that moment felt the first twinge of rebellion.

She gave him a quick, suspicious look over her shoulder, but he was smiling at her quite openly, standing there with his feet close together and his hands by his sides like a tin soldier.

The room had darkened, and in the steadily gaining light of the fire, yellow and pink in the cave of blackened bricks, the table and chairs behind them grew larger and loomed more mysteriously.

'I once lived with this woman up in Queensland,' said Madigan in a rush. 'She was sort of—hubba hubba. She wore dresses made out of hundreds of coloured scarves, and those hippy oils that make you smell like a sweet biscuit, and sandals with high heels, and her hair went right down her back, and what a voice! She used to drive me wild. I should have had a baby with her.'

'A *baby*? What's that got to do with it?'

'Isn't that what people do?' said Madigan, still standing behind her.

'It might have been once, I suppose.'

'Oh, the world hasn't changed all that much, has it?' He gave a hearty laugh. 'You, for example. You could marry some nice bloke and have a family.'

'Come off it,' she said. 'Anyway, I've had my tubes tied.'

Madigan winced.

'Want to see my scar?' She stood up, pulled out her shirt and undid the top of her jeans to show him an inch of belly.

He forced himself to cast a glance, then turned away towards the fire. It was burning merrily. He gulped. There was a pause. Scotty tucked her shirt back into her jeans and squatted down.

'Didn't leave much of a mark, did it.' His voice was colourless, but his eyes blinked violently, pressing their lashes, bending them against the glass.

'Didn't hurt, either,' said Scotty. 'Know what? Just as I went under the anaesthetic, I could hear the radio in the operating theatre. It was Simon and Garfunkel, and they were singing *Cecilia, you're breaking my heart / You're shaking my confidence daily*.' She laughed, and sang a verse. '*Makin' love in the afternoon / With Cecilia up in my bedroom / I got up to wash my face / When I come back to bed / Someone's taken my place*.'

Madigan looked at her with a twisted smile. 'Are you trying to tell me something?' he said with difficulty.

'No.' Her smile faded. 'What do you mean?'

'It doesn't matter. I just thought…'

They stared into the fire.

'I suppose you've had an abortion too, have you.' His voice was as conversational as Wally's had been at the front door.

'Two, actually. Why?'

175

'I must be old-fashioned, or something. I can't get used to it.'

'You a Catholic, are you?'

'I can make up my own mind, thanks very much.'

'I had a religious conversion when I was twenty-two,' she said. 'Baptised, confirmed the lot. It only lasted two weeks. I was an Anglican.' She laughed.

'That woman I was telling you about,' he said. 'She had very compelling eyes. Her eyes were empty of everything but compulsion.'

He moved forward and leaned his arms against the mantelpiece, so that she could not see his face. Something in the angle of his leg and foot was child-like to her: Paddle shoes, free milk at playtime.

'What'll we talk about now?' she said.

'Do you think I could stay the night?' he said in a muffled voice.

They lay on their backs like a pair of carvings on a tomb.

'The wind's getting up,' she said. 'Listen to it thumping in the chimney.'

He said nothing, but stared at the plaster garlands of the ceiling through his ugly spectacles, hands under his head.

'Aren't you going to take your glasses off?'

'Not yet.'

'Are you sleepy?'

'No.'

'I don't even know your first name,' said Scotty.

'I avoid using it. It makes me sound like a potato.'

'What is it?'

'Leo. Don't tell anyone.'

'What's wrong with that? It's Irish.'

'Go to the top of the class.'

'Wasn't there a Pope Leo?'

'Half a dozen, probably,' he said, discreetly slipping his glasses on to the floor under the bed.

'Well. Do you like your *last* name?'

'You'll try anything, won't you,' he said.

'Just want to keep things rolling along,' said Scotty. She reached out one arm and switched off the lamp. 'We don't have to fuck, if that's what's bothering you.'

He flinched. 'I thought that's what you people over here meant by inviting a bloke to stay the night.'

'It was your idea, not mine. What do you think we are, monsters? Let's go to sleep.'

He started to toss himself round in the bed, turning first his back to her and then his face with an unreadable expression on it: an angry, laughing, cynical grimace. 'I should go to sleep,' he mumbled. 'I should go home.'

'Well, go ahead! If you want to!'

'No no *no*! It's too far. I haven't got enough money for a taxi.'

'Stop thrashing round, will you? You've pulled the blankets right out at the bottom with your great feet.'

'Oh, what am I doing here?' he cried suddenly. 'I'm never going to cut the mustard over this side of the river. I go crazy at home because no one takes anything seriously except dope, and then I come over here like a humble pilgrim, cap in hand, and I get taken so seriously I nearly die, of panic, or boredom. I try to remain aloof, suspicious, sceptical and yet trusting—isn't that how it's done?' His eyes were bulging.

'How *what*'s done?' said Scotty, with an incredulous laugh.

He rounded on her. 'Well, make a joke, if you don't want me to get serious!'

'Sorry!' she said. 'I thought it *was* a joke!'

'You lot think everything's a joke.'

'*I* don't.'

'Well, don't poke fun at a bloke.'

It was like watching a war through a telescope: she could see skirmishes, wild rushes of movement to and fro, but was unable to tell whether there was a tactical intelligence in command, or whether all was lost and the armies were taking flight.

'The gulf between being awake and being asleep is *infinitesimal*,' he shouted, half mad with wakefulness, 'but it's *unbridgeable*!'

'What do you *want*?'

178

'I want to have fallen into a deep sleep five minutes ago!'

'Do you want me to tickle your back?' she said helplessly.

'I'll accept anything, at the moment.' He turned his broad, pink back to her, and she pulled up his ratty singlet and began to tickle him with her fingernails, making artistic patterns and swirls and not staying in the same place too long.

He flashed her a peculiar, almost malevolent smile over his shoulder. 'If you were a fightin' woman,' he said, 'you'd have thrown me out by now! You'd have said, "What sort of a place do you think this *is* we're running?"'

'Oh shut up smartypants,' she said, furious. 'Sleep or don't sleep. I don't care.'

There was a short silence. Then he laughed quietly, and said, 'Good on you, Scotty. Sweet dreams.'

They fell asleep at last, back to back on the hard low bed.

The kids were playing pleasantly in the kitchen. Scotty brushed Wally's hair, his fly-away white straw, and clipped Laurel's toenails, and they sat in a row in the morning sun outside the back door. Laurel got out her finger-knitting and toiled away at it, breathing heavily through her nose.

'Look, Scotty,' she said. 'I can finger-knit. But I can't make it turn round and go the other way.'

A small brisk breeze ran round the garden. Wally stumbled about on his stilts in the damp grass, singing and laughing to himself. Red leaves on top of the gum tree skittered and sparkled in the wind.

'Do you think it's going to be warm today?' said Scotty.

'Turn on the radio and find out,' said Wally sensibly.

'I feel rather happy,' said Scotty. 'It's a bit like the olden days, don't you think?'

'We weren't born in the olden days,' said Laurel, smiling at Scotty and pushing her glasses up her nose with the back of her wrist. 'So we don't know. Do we.'

Scotty crept back into her room and stood at the table. When she turned round she saw that Madigan was awake, lying on his back watching her with his eyes half-closed. Without his spectacles, the whole area of skin round his eyes looked tender and defenceless; his lips were dark red, his pale cheeks blurred with a shimmer of new whisker.

'You look funny,' he said, 'standing there in that position.'

'Funny?'

'Yes. You sort of pull your mouth down and it gives you a double chin.'

'Thanks a lot.'

'Was I really unbearable last night?'

'No more than you are this morning.'

'What've I said?'

'I love being told I've got a double chin and look funny.'

'You're tough enough to take the truth, aren't you?'

'I *know* the truth already,' she said, 'about the way I look.'

'Sometimes you look real pretty. And other times your face is…kind of…lumpy.'

'I *know* all this! You don't have to tell me! I don't think I'm beautiful!'

'I'm not either,' he said. 'I know I'm just a clod who can play the mouth organ.'

'I *like* the way you look.'

He pulled a frog-face and laughed. 'Cut it out, Scotty. You make me feel like a matinee idol.'

'How did we get on to this subject, anyway?' she said.

'I was just watching you. I like you, Scotty. Come here.'

She took two steps towards the bed and he flung himself at her knees and tumbled her down beside him. She fell stiffly. 'Come on,' he said. 'Put your head on my shoulder. That's right. Don't take too much notice of me. I'm in shock, a lot of the time. Come on, leave your head there. People ought to be able to be nice to each other sometimes. Not crying, are you?'

'I don't know,' she said. 'There's some funny liquid coming out my eyes.'

He felt her face with his fingertips. 'I think they're tears, Scotty.'

She started to laugh in weak, silly fits, and he kept holding her head gently between his neck and shoulder.

'Ruth's going to leave, I think,' she said, 'and she'll take Laurel with her.'

'Isn't the boy hers too?'

'Yes. But Laurel's been *mine*.'

'Oh. I get it.'

'I thought you didn't understand new-fangled ideas.'

'I know what it is to like a *kid*, for Christ's sake.'

The sun was slanting through the faded pink curtains, making the wooden floor hum with brightness.

'Want me to read you a story?' he said.

'All right.'

He picked up a book from beside the bed and looked at its cover. It was one of Laurel's. *'The Juniper Tree,'* he announced in a state school 'interesting' voice. 'Let's read a page each. I'll start. *It was a long time ago now, as much as two thousand years maybe, that there was a rich man and he had a wife and she was beautiful and good, and they loved each other very much but they had no children...'*

When it was her turn she feared to offend with her unpopular tone of voice, but he suddenly seized her head in both hands and kissed her violently on the mouth. 'What a nice voice you've got!' he said. 'I've never really heard it before.'

'It's a teacher's voice,' she said.

'I love it,' he said casually. 'My turn. *She began to hate the little boy and would push him around from one corner to the other and push him here and pinch him there so that the poor child was always in a fright. When he came home from school there was no quiet place where he could be.*'

'This is a bit close to the bone,' said Scotty.

'It's only a simple story,' he said, looking up and marking his place with one finger.

'That's what's so terrible about it,' said Scotty. 'It's so ordinary and familiar.' She tried to wipe the tears away surreptitiously with the corner of the sheet.

'Bear up, Scotty!'

'Aren't I allowed to cry at a sad story?'

'Of course you are.' He read on to the end, singing the little song each time—'*Tweet twee what a pretty bird am I!*'—in his cracked, true voice, glancing at her to see how she was taking it. Scotty wept away soundlessly, head between his elbow and his side, holding the sheet up to her eyes.

When the story was finished he put down the book and they lay there quietly in the bed. In the next room someone had begun to play the piano, hesitantly and with many a mistake. Madigan shifted so that his head was on her breast and she held it in her arms.

*

Ruth set off with her long, swagman's stride that Saturday morning, through the network of streets and lanes to Dennis's place. A heavy string bag stuffed with clothes and food was slung over her shoulder. Her head, borne well forward on her bowed neck, cut the air with a patient expression, her eyes half squinted against the breeze of her progress. She was thinking sketchily, in a mild, scattered panic, that she would soon have to start looking for another place to live.

She remembered the night she and Scotty had ridden their bikes to the empty house Scotty had found. They had pulled loose one of the louvres of the bathroom window and crammed themselves through the gap, breathless with stifled giggling and the intruder's voluptuous desire to shit. The torch's custardy ring of light wavered before them in the pitch-dark rooms, fleas swarmed and attacked their shins.

'What do you reckon?' said Scotty, standing the torch on the cement floor so that their ankles were bathed in its beam.

Ruth hesitated. 'I dunno. Without the others… two's not enough, is it?'

'I think I might know a bloke,' said Scotty.

Three had not been enough. Still, in the yard, sometimes a weird spasm occurred in Ruth's nervous system which almost passed for emotion. Her spade bit and spat. Weeds gave up their grip with a rending sound. Her mop steamed gently in morning sunlight;

184

her arms reached up with pegs and sopping cloth. Moons speckled the concrete under the nectarine tree, and bounced off the brick wall of the shed, bright as day. The sighs and protests that weather wrung from the house were to Ruth like the familiar creak of knee or wrist. She would have to drag herself out, gather herself together once more, draw the children round her like a warm but prickling blanket, and take the leap, start it all again, make what she could of bare rooms and a backyard full of dry clods.

A red car flew past Ruth where she trudged. She glanced into it and saw, like a frozen scene from a play, a Greek man driving, intent at once on the road and on his wife who was telling a story with upflung hand and merry, moving lips. A child leaned over between them from the back seat, like his father listening eagerly, rapt, mouth trembling, ready to burst into laughter. They performed their happy moment for her and were gone. She stood on the corner waiting for the lights to change.

She came in the back way and found Dennis in bed at midday in his stuffy room, unconscious, though he swore later that he had merely been asleep. He was curled up on his side, his mouth agape so that the pillow was soaked with saliva in a wide ring under his cheek. The gas fire was on full blast, the window nailed shut, the blankets sodden with sweat. Ruth stepped forward in alarm to make sure he was still actually breathing.

She turned the heater down to a mere hiss and opened the front door to let in a stream of sunny air. Still he did not move. She stood staring down at him, saw his blond hair all damp and sticking to his skull, his eyes tightly closed, his thick lashes, much darker than his hair, gummed together in spikes on the grey circles under his eyes. She went out into the daylight and bought a bag of oranges at the shop. When she got back he had not stirred. His boots lay where he had wrenched them off, one standing upright, the other crumpled over and drooping at the ankle. The sight of them provoked an irritable tenderness in her: she put her hand on his forehead and he rolled over suddenly on to his back. His eyes popped open and he stared blindly at her.

'G'day.'

'You're not looking *after* yourself properly!' she said angrily. 'You're *sick*!'

His greyish-blue eyes contracted; he looked puzzled. 'Mouth's all dry,' he mumbled.

She got out her pocket knife, cut up an orange into eighths and served it to him on the folded paper bag. He did not notice that she gave him three oranges in this manner, but went on greedily sucking the slices and dropping the peels among the screwed-up tissues beside the bed. He announced his draconian cure in a voice she hardly recognised. 'I'm gunna sweat it outa me system,' he grunted.

'We better forget about the Prom, then,' said Ruth.

186

He did not answer, but flopped back on to the pillow and closed his eyes. Roughly she pushed his head to one side and flipped the pillow over.

She stayed with him all day, as he burned away in the bed, sometimes laughing childishly to himself or champing his jaws as if chewing. Once he half sat up and saw her sitting there and let out what sounded like a sob. 'Oh, hullo sweetheart!' he said, and dozed off again. Towards late afternoon he was sleeping more gently, and his temperature had dropped.

She cleaned up his dismal kitchen, emptied food out of its packets into airtight jars and lined them up in the wire-fronted meat-safe which served him as a cupboard. At ten o'clock she went into the bathroom and cleaned her teeth, brushing noisily with the water running. She turned off the tap and the silence it left was filled with the quiet sound of rain.

When she woke at six in the morning, his skin felt cool and dry. She put one arm carefully round his back and lay there in the dim tingling of hope, the optimism of simply existing, that comes sometimes to the wakeful one in a house where others are sleeping. She heard the wind cradling the house, moving endlessly in the concrete spaces of his yard.

In the afternoon the sky was clear and the air had stilled. Dennis would not stay in bed, though his face was shadowy with thinness.

They came into the gardens at the top corner where the big eucalypts stand becalmed, their bark wrinkled at the junction of trunk and branch like human skin after an idle winter. On the northern horizon, beyond the city, there gathered mighty palaces of cloud, pale Italian pink and of complex, fat design.

No, Dennis would not do it.

'What's wrong with the way things are now?' he said, sliding out his chin and twisting his head about as if he were wearing a tight collar.

'You don't look after yourself,' said Ruth.

'Oh, yesterday!' He clicked his tongue. 'That was nothing. That was different.'

'I dunno,' said Ruth. 'Sometimes people need—'

'I don't wanna get married!'

'I didn't mean that!' she cried. 'I never meant married! You *know* that's not what I meant!'

'Well,' he said sullenly. 'I don't wanna *live* with anyone, either. With a woman, I mean.'

'Why not.' Her voice was already dull with defeat, but she slogged on.

'You know what happens to couples! What do you bloody women talk about in these groups, anyway!'

'There hasn't *been* a group for two years,' said Ruth.

'Find another woman to live with, why don't you, if you don't like the set-up you're in now.' He threw up one hand and glanced after it, as if hoping for a materialisation. 'Find one with kids—you'd get the full sympathy syndrome.'

'I don't want to,' said Ruth. 'I want to live with *you*.'

'I can't.'

'But *why*?'

He punched one fist into the other palm and said in exasperation, 'Time. Time, mostly.'

'What do you mean, time.'

'I haven't *got* any. I go to work, I go to meetings.' He turned his face away, almost laughing with embarrassment.

'We'd have *more* time, if we lived in the same house,' she said, flogging the hopeless argument.

'Look, Ru. If you wanted more than what you're already gettin', you'd have to ask me to give up *politics*.' He threw down his trump card with a defiant flourish, watching her out of the tail of his eye.

Ruth's head came up, as he had foreseen. 'Oh, I'd never do *that*,' she said, chastened.

They sat opposite each other at a weathered timber table under creepers thronged with green and yellowing leaves, a tray of Devonshire tea between them. Ruth was almost crying, fumbling for her tobacco.

'I mean—you see blokes,' said Dennis, frowning and grinning and forcing the spoon again and again into the sugar bowl, 'blokes who walk round as if they've got a sack of cement on their shoulders, and the woman's sittin' there full of resentment, and he's wishin' he could—'

'That's not what I *meant*,' said Ruth again, in misery. 'I meant—it'd be *collective*. Not like a couple. We'd have separate rooms—'

'Nah, Ru. It's not on, mate. Giss a scone.'

She shoved the plate towards him and they ate, a caricature of the couples around them, unable to look at each other. She felt stuffed with food, and ate to comfort herself, though she could hardly swallow. A wasp dived repeatedly into the jam dish, then fled sideways. They eyed it, nervous of its sting. 'Shit! Oh, shit!' said Dennis, swatting, a small blob of whipped cream on the end of his nose.

They walked round the lake, wading through oceans of dead leaves. The gardens were as busy as Bourke Street: whole Jewish families, parties of nuns and old people from institutions moved along the curving paths, gesturing graciously and casting their eyes to left and right like courtly dancers. There was no hope for the human race. Everything would end in greyness.

'Oh, come on, Ru. Cheer up!' said Dennis, dropping an arm across her shoulders.

'People always say that to me,' she said bitterly, in a low voice.

'No they don't. Come on,' he insisted. He hugged her shoulders till they cracked, then gave her a hard thump between the shoulder blades. 'I'm with you all the way,' he said, and put his hands back in his pockets.

'Why don't you come round more then.'

He could hardly hear her. 'What?'

'I said, *Come round more*!' she yelled at him. 'You reckon you're on my side, but you're never there, except to sleep.'

He writhed his shoulders. 'I don't like it at your place,' he said. 'I don't feel comfortable there. Scotty puts me off.'

'She puts me off, too,' said Ruth. 'I *hate* her.' She looked almost noble with wretchedness. 'She's always tellin' me what to do.'

'Kick her out then.'

'I'd rather go myself. I've got *some* pride.'

'I'll help you, soon as you get a place,' he said, safe enough now to be generous.

'Thanks,' said Ruth dully.

She saw a dead sparrow lying half covered in leaves at the corner of a garden bed, and gave it a kick with the toe of her shoe. The little corpse flipped up oddly, its wings stiffly spread, and dived back headfirst into the thick, papery carpet. She glanced crookedly at Dennis, as guilty as if she had killed the bird herself, but he had witnessed the display of sadism with a half laugh of respect, even of comradeliness. She began to talk in a rush.

'The kids used to always have funerals for dead animals,' she said. 'Laurel used to make little crosses for the graves, 'n' everything. Then when the budgies started keelin' over from old age, first they had mass graves, then the kids got sick of it, 'n' the last one that died, Wal just chucked it in the bushes.'

Dennis laughed out loud in relief. 'That's the spirit. Good on you,' he said, as if admiring a skilful performance.

Ruth laughed without mirth. 'Next thing you'll be sayin' "Well done", like Scotty does,' she said. 'Talkin' like a teacher.' She tightened her lips and mimicked Scotty: '*Well done!*'

She took another breath, but before she could speak again he had veered off the path and wandered down to the edge of the lake. He crouched there above the burnished surface of the water, looking for fish perhaps, and she stood watching him from behind, her arms wrapped round herself. In that moment she saw him separate from herself, forgetful of her, about to emerge whole into the outside world. She fell back weakly into love with his past, with the things he knew which she did not. She loved him and would appropriate for her own son the accoutrements of this idealised working-class boyhood: bare laminex tables, sagging single beds with heads made of curved iron, cheap tartan slippers, slug guns, grey tube-like shorts, playgrounds ringing with harsh cries and encircled by peppercorns and cyclone wire. The tears shrivelled in her chest: the temper of her blood was already adjusted.

*

Scotty knew, when Wally stuck out his tongue at her at the bottom of the stairs, that Ruth must be back. There was new resolution in the air, in Ruth's firm step and grim, purposeful expression; at dinner time people kept their eyes on their plates, embarrassed at the possibility of conversation. Only Wally seemed relaxed and oblivious of tension.

'Hey Lol,' he said, shoving a handful of rice into his mouth. 'You know that kid Sharon that I fucked?'

'You?' Laurel blushed. 'You never fucked anyone! You're too little.'

'I—*did*!' shouted Wally. His cheeks were greasy with food. 'Down the creek! Me 'n' her—'

'That'll do,' cut in Ruth. 'Eat your dinner. Here, Wal. Use a fork.' She pushed one into his fist. Wally looked up with his squinting grin.

'Wanna know somethink?' His smile became secretive. 'We might be movin' out. An' if we do, it'll be because of *someone*.' He ran his triumphant eyes round the assembled household. Horrified, they stared at him. Wally glowed and blossomed. 'Someone at *this table*,' he said. 'Someone *fat*, with sorta black *hair*.' His eyes came to rest on Scotty; he raised one rice-smeared

193

hand and pointed at her. 'It's *you*, Scotty! 'Cause you treat us like *shit*!'

Wally and Scotty stared at each other. Alex and Ruth dropped their eyes, excruciated lest someone laugh.

'An' Alex, too!' shouted Wally, angry now as he felt the transitoriness of his moment of power. ''Cause *he* made us *eat cod*!'

Laurel cried out in indignation. 'You never told me, Ruth!'

'I was gunna, mate,' she said wearily.

'Won't we have a meeting?' said Alex.

There was a pause.

'I don't think we need to have a meeting,' said Ruth, staring with eyes of glass at the wall beside Alex's head. 'There's nothin' to say. Only a few loose ends to tie up.'

'You mean—it's all settled?' said Alex.

'It's time to get out,' said Ruth. 'I wish I'd gone last year.'

There was a run of movement round the table. Laurel turned to Ruth again and said, shocked and excited, 'We'll have to find a really good house, won't we, Ruth! What sort of house will we find?'

'Oh, nothin' special, matey,' said Ruth with a sharp sigh. 'Just s'long's it's a roof over our heads.'

With one accord Ruth and Scotty got up to clear the plates. They skirted each other widely in the confined space, their faces stiff with shame and hatred. People ate their desserts in haste, standing up in different parts of the room.

Ruth led the children into the lounge and turned on the television. It flickered at them where they sat in tight formation on the couch, Ruth in the middle with an arm around each child. On the screen a jet took off in California with a stuntman rigged up and strapped erect to its top.

'That's Spiderman,' said Laurel. She stuck her thumb in her mouth.

'No it's not,' said Wally. 'That's the Human Fly.'

The man's face must have been hideously stretched with the pressure of the air.

'Ruth,' said Wally.

'What, mate.'

'You know Jimmy. Well when's he comin' back?' 'Cause I miss him *so much*.'

She squeezed him harder against her side, feeling the springy give of his little rib-cage.

'We should be hearin' from him any day now,' she said.

'Yeah, but *when*.' He was quite loose against her.

'I told you, Wal. Any day.'

Laurel took her thumb out. 'Ruth,' she said. 'What does the Human Fly do when he's finished?'

'Collects his pay cheque and goes home, I suppose,' said Ruth.

In the kitchen Scotty and Alex washed and dried the dishes, without speaking. Scotty passed the lounge room door on her way to the stairs, and glanced in. Laurel's head was the only one to turn. She looked straight at Scotty, and moved her left hand, on the arm of the couch, in a furtive salute.

*

Over the river, Scotty walked straight into the sepulchral house, past the foot of the stairs and towards the kitchen, from which conversation could be heard. She paused outside the door.

'I think we should allow for each other's idiosyncrasies,' said a man's voice, slightly raised.

'Each other's what?' said a woman.

'Do you mean laziness, Tony?' said another woman.

'There's no need to get *personal*,' said the man.

'How can you talk about idiosyncrasies and not be personal?' said the second woman.

'I think you're being a bit sharp with me,' said Tony, sounding wounded.

Scotty let herself be seen in the doorway. It was a dim room whose window was half-obscured by ivy, and no one had turned on the light, though some activity seemed to be in progress. A tall man who had rubberbanded his hair into a tight little club at the back of his neck was crossing the room holding in his fist a bunch of what looked like flowers: he passed Scotty and she saw that they were cooked sausages. Madigan was not present. The sausage-eater was drowning his food in tomato sauce and paid her no attention, but one of the women looked up at her and smiled.

'I was looking for Madigan,' said Scotty.

'He's out in his room, I think,' said Myra. 'Like a cup of tea?'

'No thank you,' said Scotty. 'I don't drink tea.'

'Don't you?' said Myra pleasantly. 'What do you do all day, then?'

Scotty would not admit Myra's gentle joke. She stood by the fridge with her hands plunged into the pockets of her zipper jacket, her eyes travelling warily round the room, her dark face cold with shyness, ready to judge.

'Which is his room?' she said.

'Out the back, past the dunny, and keep going,' said Myra.

The shed was shut. She knocked.

'What.'

She opened the door and slid in. He was lying under an eiderdown with a book open on his chest. He stared at her. The small area of room which was not bed had a temporary look, clogged with things half-unpacked from boxes, as if he had just arrived or was contemplating leaving. There did not appear to be any source of light, or air.

197

'You'll go blind,' said Scotty, 'trying to read in that light.'

'I'm hiding in here,' he said.

'Have you got your *pyjamas* on? At seven o'clock at night?'

'None of your business.'

'What are you hiding from?'

'Oh, the women want us to wash up more, and do the shopping.'

She grabbed the corner of the eiderdown and whisked it off him. 'Get to the kitchen then, bludger.' He was revealed on his back, fully dressed, with his hands up holding the book in front of his chin.

'What *is* this?' he cried in a rage, not moving. 'The rape of the Sabine women? You come bursting in here while a bloke's trying to have a quiet read—is nothing sacred?'

'Oh bugger it,' she said, turning away from the bed with a gesture of disgust. 'I've got enough house problems without sticking my nose into yours.'

'You're so rude!'

'Am I? Sorry.' She sat down on a stool. 'I feel terrible. I don't know what to do with myself. I just hopped on the bus and came over. Want to come out for a coffee, or something? I promise I'll be nice. Not manful.'

'Give me a minute to think about it.'

'I'll pay, even.'

'Let me *think*, will you?'

'Entertain me, for God's sake! I'll be crazy in ten minutes. Go on—I helped you, the other night.'

'You call that help?' he scoffed. 'I'll never forgive you for that night. I felt—contemptuous.'

'*What?*'

'You were pathetic. You were so forgiving you nearly made me sick. You should've kicked me out.'

'Oh I should have, should I?'

She stood at the end of his bed looking down at his heavy crumpled figure, his thick mousy hair and resentful expression, and suddenly hurled herself on him, sending the book flying. She straddled him, grabbed a handful of his shirt front and wrenched at it violently. There was a satisfying sound of ripping cloth, and buttons peppered the wall.

'Hey!' he roared, electrified. 'I *liked* that shirt!'

'Stiff shit.' She pinned his shoulders to the bed and pounded him against the mattress till his teeth rattled, but he recovered his wits and got her leg in a lock: she fought hard, but the best she could do was to keep the upper half of him immobilised, and by now they were weak with laughter and effort.

'You know what you are, Scotty?' he gasped. 'You're a star-fucker.'

'Who, me? You flea-bitten mutt.' She could only dig her fingers into his shoulders, deadlocked as they were.

199

'Why didn't you kick me out?'

'Because you looked as if you wanted to stay.'

'I was bored!'

'Bored! Bored, were you? Well, fuck you! If you were bored, why didn't you say so, and go elsewhere?'

He looked abashed, and slid his eyes sideways. 'I was shy.'

'Oi was shoi,' she mimicked him. 'Why don't you just work out what you want to do, and then do it?'

'I thought I had—but suddenly I found you tickling my back.'

'I didn't hear any complaints at the time.'

'How could I complain? It was like sleeping with the district nurse!'

She let go and so did he, and she stood up, still panting, and tucked her shirt in at the waist.

'Come on,' she said. 'Let's go and have a coffee.'

'I haven't got much money,' he said automatically.

'I've got plenty. Come on.'

'Don't rush me, Scotty! You're so precipitate.' He got off the bed and scrounged under it for his shoes, which he pulled on and began to lace up in a complicated fashion.

She stood by the door waiting.

'Actually,' said Madigan, as he finished tying a bow in the first shoelace and turned his attention to the other, 'I can't really go out for a coffee. There's something I have to do.'

'What?'

'Sing.'

'Tonight?'

'Yes. In this old folkie club up the top of Collins Street. It's the sort of joint where earnest young chaps play those guitars that don't make any noise.'

'Why didn't you say so before?' she said impatiently.

'Well, it's like this,' he said, settling into a leisurely exposition. 'The pay's a bit piddling, but it's a foot in the door, as it were. I've got a couple of things planned— few jokes, few songs—bee-yodle-ay-i-hew!' he warbled in his sweet, sharp voice. 'I am a professional, after all.'

He stood up slowly and combed his hair down with both hands. 'It's not very gentlemanly, is it,' he added politely, 'keeping you hanging on like this.'

Scotty pointed the toe of one foot and described a figure of eight on the lino, her hands out of sight inside her jacket. 'Well, I suppose I ought to push off, then,' she said.

'You couldn't give us a lift into town, could you?' said Madigan, glancing around him on the floor.

She looked up at him with narrowed eyes. 'I told you,' she said in a blank voice. 'I came on the bus.'

'Oh. Never mind, then. I'll jump on the tram myself. Better get a move on,' he said, unconvincingly.

He buttoned his black corduroy jacket right up to the neck to cover his torn shirt and stood at the foot of the bed, as if on parade.

Scotty gave a short laugh. 'You look like a Jew at a funeral.'

'You wouldn't want to come with me, I suppose,' he said, not looking at her.

They got off the tram at the Town Hall and walked up Collins Street in the fresh dark. Leaves were coming down here, too: big twisted ones that crackled underfoot on the square pavement blocks, or drifted crabwise with a loud scraping sound.

In the window of an expensive shop, Scotty noticed a diaphanous flowery dress.

'Look,' she said, pointing. 'If I were that kind of person, that's the sort of dress I'd love to wear.'

'You're not, though, are you,' he said with a gusty laugh. 'Imagine you! With your big fat body and crabby face.'

She walked on quickly. He caught up with her on the steps of the Alexandra Club, where she sat between the polished brass handrails, her face expressionless. He took hold of her hand.

'Hey Scotty,' he said gently. 'Do you want me to live with you?'

'No!' she cried, trying to jerk her hand away.

He kept his grip on it, and gave it a little shake. 'What aristocratic fingers you have, Scotty,' he said.

'We don't even know each other,' said Scotty.

'But isn't that why people live together? So they *can* know each other?'

'How should I know?'

'I thought you people knew all about this kind of thing.'

'I find you extremely…disturbing,' she said.

'Oh! Well…I'll have to think about that,' he said. He dropped her hand and mooned away towards the top of the street. 'You have a decent job, of course. And I'm just the king of the dole bludgers.'

'You play for money, don't you? I thought you said you were a professional.'

'I *know*,' he snapped. 'I know, I know, I know.'

She shrugged and stood up from the cold step, plucking at the seat of her pants.

He dawdled more than usual, at the end, and when they left the building and he stood back for her at the door it was as if she were dragging him behind her. A cool wind raced up Collins Street.

'I loved the music,' she said awkwardly. 'I loved it in there. I was really surprised. The songs were beautiful. You've got a beautiful voice.'

'Don't flatter me!' he yelled, almost choking.

'I'm not! I liked the music!'

'They're only period pieces! I thought you were supposed to be intelligent! Can't you *see* that?'

'I just wanted to say I was happy in there!'

'OK! OK! I'm glad you were happy!' He jerked his big head away from her.

'What are we going to do now?' said Scotty.

'I wish you had a car,' he said. 'I feel like being waited on hand and foot.'

'Well I haven't. We'll have to get the tram, or walk.'

He stopped in his tracks and turned on her so suddenly that his shoulder jarred her chin and her teeth clashed. 'I'd like to be brutally frank with you, Scotty,' he said.

'What?'

'I think you're wasting your time with me.'

She stared at him.

'I'm a cold fish sometimes,' he said. 'Specially after a gig.'

'What are you trying to say?' She might have been looking at him from twenty yards away.

Again that run of expressions passed across his face, like the shuffling of not-quite identical cards: malevolence, dislike, a sarcastic smile. 'You want to take me home with you, don't you?' he said.

'I suppose so. Don't you want to come?'

'Why did you come to this gig, Scotty?'

'To hear you sing! You invited me!'

'Yes—but I can't be responsible, see what I mean? It's work, for me. Work first, women second. I can't be responsible for you having a good time.'

'I don't know what you're talking about,' said Scotty. 'And I think that kind of priority system is absolutely pathetic.'

They faced each other under the trees. The foliage shifted about restlessly, veiling and revealing the street lamp. Stubbornly he pressed on.

'When you go to those rock gigs, like the one I met you at—what do you go for?'

'What are you *talking* about?'

He shuffled his feet impatiently and turned his face into the wind: it flattened his hair and he looked smaller, as if standing inside a casing of garments too large for him. 'Look—before I talked to you, that night you and Alex drove me home, I was standing at the bar in that awful dump, and there was a girl next to me, pretty, but you could hardly see her face, it was so caked with make-up. One of the blokes in Alex's band walks up to the bar—that thin tall bloke with hair slicked back and trousers hitting the shoe just right, you know? And she turns and says to him in this dead voice, "Do you come here often?" And the bloke goes, "That's not a very original approach." And she keeps staring at him and says, "What?" I mean, Scotty, do you get it? She'd never even heard the joke. Oh Jesus!' he groaned, gnashing his teeth and butting his shoulder against the wall. 'They were like two corpses. I can't stand it.'

'What's all this got to do with *me*?'

'You go to those gigs, don't you? Looking for someone to go home with?'

'Where are you *getting* all this stuff from? I've never picked up a bloke in my life!' She was facing him, four-square.

He looked shocked, then nonplussed; he spun round, clapped his hands together like a master of ceremonies, and suddenly looked uncannily suave.

'Sex,' he declared, 'is a nuisance.'

'But it makes you feel good.'

'So does a Choo-Choo Bar.'

'Not *that* good.'

Way down at the bottom of the street appeared the headlights and illuminated number of a tram. 'Listen,' she said. 'If you're about to have a fit of the vapours, I'm going.'

He seized her arm. '*I don't want you to go.*'

'Lay off, will you?' She fought free and took two steps back. 'You make me feel crazy. I don't understand what you want from me.'

'Sometimes,' he said, turning humble, 'I think what I'm looking for is a surrogate mother—someone to cuddle me and tell me there's no such thing as duty—nothing I have to do.'

'You won't get that from me!' The rails were singing shrilly two blocks away. 'I thought you'd been around,' she said, talking quickly and feeling for her money. 'I didn't think you were one of those junior woodchucks. You told me you were a professional. I thought you'd been *around*.'

'I'm just a babe in the woods, compared to you!'

The sign on the tram was visible now. It was the right one. It swayed up the hill, cord lashing in the wind, the driver black in his cabin.

'You don't feel comfortable with me, do you,' he insisted. 'I wish you did. I wish I could make you feel comfortable.'

She was halfway across the road to the tramline, flagging the driver down as if afraid she was invisible.

'Why'd you do it, Scotty!' he cried out wildly. 'All that stuff.'

'Do *what*?' Her incredulous face flashed at him over her shoulder. 'What are you crying for?'

His words were drowned in the screeching of the tram's arrival. Scotty was up the step in one bound and into a seat before it had properly stopped. The conductor grinned at her and dinged the bell so that the tram lurched away again without a pause and went keeling round the corner. Madigan stood there between the silvery tracks staring after her: she hung her head out the open doorway and waved, but she was already too far away for him to see her face. She could have been anyone. And probably was. He clenched his teeth and let out a subdued shriek, rolling his oyster eyes to heaven and punching downwards from the waist with both fists. Then he turned rapidly aside, crossed back to the footpath, and sloped off towards Swanston Street. By the time he had passed Georges he was singing to himself.

*

Ruth came home from the movies at midnight. She opened the front door, then went back to the car and carried the sleeping children in to their beds, one at a time. She put out her hand to the knob of her own door, and noticed the folded sheet of paper half in the room and half out, on the floor. She bent down and picked it up.

It was one of Scotty's self-portraits: a stumpy figure in baggy pants, a blue and white striped jumper and tiny black sunglasses. The figure was wearing a penitent expression and holding a white flag. Out of its mouth came a balloon containing the words *Let's bury the hatchet*.

Ruth heaved a slow, quivering sigh, stepped into her room, and shut the door. The note aroused in her such a wave of loathing and disgust that she thought she was going to be sick: she slouched to the fireplace and leaned her forehead against the cold bricks. After a moment she sat down on the bed and pulled her diary out from under the mattress.

Scotty, lying awake in the dark, her ears sharpened by a kind of dreary hope, heard Ruth unfold the note and sigh.

In the morning Ruth was already in the yard when Scotty came out to make her breakfast.

'Hey Ruth,' she called into the yard where Ruth was upending the compost bucket into the enclosure she had built with planks. 'Want me to make you a cup of camomile tea?'

'Yes please,' said Ruth, without looking up.

Scotty fiddled with the latch of the wire door. 'How do you make it?' This was as close as Scotty would ever come to appeasement.

Ruth did not give an inch. She turned round in a slow movement, holding the green plastic bucket in her arms, and stared narrowly at Scotty. 'You've made it before.'

Scotty stood still. Then she shrugged, let the wire door slam loosely shut, and went to the sink where she began to fill a yellow saucepan with water.

Ruth came into the kitchen from outside.

'Did you get my note?' said Scotty.

Ruth raised her eyes. Her mouth was a bitter line.

'Do you really think,' she said slowly and deliberately, 'that a little note with a smart drawing is gunna make any difference at all, at this stage?'

Scotty withdrew, stiff-backed.

'I've felt your hatchet too many times to drop mine for *a funny drawing*,' said Ruth.

Scotty pushed past her and out the screen door into the yard. She began to unpeg dry sheets from the line, slinging them over her shoulder. Somewhere inside the house a bell was ringing in a sharp, double rhythm. The pegs dropped into the grass and disappeared. The bell stopped. She elbowed her way in through the door and met Ruth in the middle of the room. Sun laid its bland stripes across the scarred red concrete floor.

'That was Jimmy,' said Ruth in a queer, faint voice. 'He's comin' back. They let him out. He asked me when he could take—'

'Oh Ruth.'

For one beat of time there might have been comfort offered, accepted, a quick flooding over the barricades: but Ruth stepped back instead of forward, folding her arms and narrowing her eyes. The air sang in the room.

'Ruth,' said Scotty in a trembling voice. 'I'm finding life very difficult at the moment. Can't we try to be a bit more pleasant to each other, just till you go?'

Ruth fixed her with a terrible white stare. 'Sometimes the simplest things are the hardest to do.'

'But if we could just make an effort—'

'I don't *feel* like being particularly pleasant to you, Scotty,' said Ruth between her teeth.

Scotty swallowed. 'Maybe we could try to be civil to each other.'

'I'm being *bloody* civil to you! You know what I hate about you, Scotty? You've never really been up

210

against it. All your life you've just taken what you need. Everything all falls into place for you. You don't even know what trouble is, or grief.'

Scotty lashed back. 'So now there's a Richter scale of suffering, is there? They'll have to extend it right up as far as martyrdom and sainthood in your case, won't they.'

Ruth's teeth cut her breath. 'You fuckin' cold bitch,' she whispered.

'Christ, Ruth, you make me feel—'

What was this?

They were on opposite sides of the room, the two women, footsoles spreading on stone, backs against walls. Sheets floated like flags or slowly falling banners, a chair sprawled on its side, a plate struck a window-frame and smashed brilliantly, ears roared like oceans, sweat popped out in diamond chips. There was a loud noise. It was a voice screeching 'Old! Old! Old!'

There fell a silence. Chooks crooned and clucked drowsily, tapped their silly beaks against the tin fence. A fly laboured.

So this was why people in real life screamed and broke things and grew violent: because the mind let go, and afterwards your body was as loose and fine as a sleeper's, a dancer's, a satisfied lover's. You were empty, all your molecules were harmoniously realigned. You were skinned, liberated, wise. You were out of reach.

A mouth formed words. 'Now we can leave each other alone.'

'I can accept that,' said another, low, a thousand miles away.

212

Text Classics

textclassics.com.au